Seven  O'Clock Tales

Enid Blyton

Seven O'Clock Tales

mammoth

First published in Great Britain 1943
by Methuen & Co Ltd
This edition first published1991 by Dean
Published 1993 by Mammoth
Reissued 2000 by Mammoth
an imprint of Egmont Children's Books Limited,
a division of Egmont Holding Limited
239 Kensington High Street, London W8 6SA

ISBN 0 7497 1339 9

10 9 8 7 6 5 4 3

A CIP catalogue record for this title
is available from the British Library

Printed in Great Britain
by Cox & Wyman Ltd, Reading, Berkshire

CONTENTS

The Enchanted Shoelace

There was once a little pixie called Skippy who went shopping in his village. As he trotted along his shoelace broke and his shoe came undone.

'Bother!' said Skippy, stopping. 'Now I must buy another shoelace.'

But he didn't need to buy one – for as he went merrily along he saw one lying in the road. His shoes were red, and the lace was green, but that didn't matter. It would lace up his shoe, whatever colour it was!

He slipped the lace into his shoe and tied it. That was fine. Now he was quite all right. Off he went again, skipping along, as happy as a bumble-bee.

Soon he came to a sweet shop and he looked in very longingly. He hadn't any money for sweets – but how delicious those big peppermints did look, to be sure!

'I just wish I had a pocketful of those!' sighed Skippy, and on he went. In a short while he felt something heavy in his pocket, and he put in his hand to feel what it was.

Peppermints! Peppermints by the dozen! Ooh, what a surprise! But however did they come there?

'My wish came true!' marvelled little Skippy. 'Oh, what a wonderful thing!'

He didn't know that he had a magic shoelace in his shoe – a lace that had once belonged to a witch and was enchanted! It came undone and nearly tripped him up.

'Bother!' said Skippy, doing it up. But he couldn't be cross for long with a pocketful of peppermints. He saw a little white kitten playing with its tail in the sunshine. Skippy was very fond of animals and he stood and watched it.

'I do wish I had a little white kitten just like that!' he said.

'Miaow!' Something rubbed against his legs, and Skippy looked down. He saw another little white kitten, looking up at him and mewing.

'Bless me!' said Skippy, in astonishment. 'If that isn't another wish come true! Well, well, well!'

He picked up the kitten and cuddled it. It nestled happily under his coat, glad to belong to a nice little pixie like Skippy. He bent down and did up his shoelace which had again come undone.

'This is really very strange,' thought the

pixie, tickling the kitten under the chin. 'This must be my lucky day, or something. I wonder if another wish will come true.'

He blinked his eyes and thought hard. 'I wish my suit was made of gold!' he said.

In a flash Skippy's red suit changed to a gleaming yellow. He was dressed in gold!

'Ooh!' said Skippy, amazed. 'Look at me all dressed up in gold! I'm a prince! I'm as grand as can be!'

His shoelace came undone again, and trailed on the ground. 'Bother!' said Skippy. 'It will trip me up as sure as eggs are eggs!'

He did it up, feeling most excited. He must tell somebody about his great good fortune. He would go to his friend Tickler the gnome and tell him. How surprised Tickler would be! Aha, he would wish all kinds of things for Tickler the gnome!

Off he went, skipping down the road as gaily as could be. What a day! What an adventure!

He banged at Tickler's door and the gnome opened it in surprise, staring at Skippy and the kitten.

'Why do you knock so hard?' he asked. 'Oh, Skippy – how beautiful you look! Where did you get that fine suit made of gold?'

'Would *you* like one?' asked Skippy, beaming.

'All right! I wish you had a suit like mine, Tickler!'

Hey presto! At once the gnome shone brightly in a suit as fine as Skippy's. He stared down at himself in amazement.

'Oh, Skippy!' he said. 'Skippy! What's happened? Do your wishes all come true?'

'Yes,' said Skippy, happily, and he stepped forward to go into Tickler's house. But his shoelace was undone again and nearly tripped him up. 'Bother, bother, bother!' he said, and did it up. Then he went into Tickler's neat little house.

'I can't tell you why my wishes come true,' he said to Tickler. 'They just suddenly did.'

'But there must be some reason why,' said Tickler, puzzled. 'Have you anything new on you, Skippy?'

'No, nothing,' said Skippy, quite forgetting about the shoelace. 'The magic just suddenly came.'

'Wish something else,' said Tickler. 'Wish for a jolly good dinner!'

'I wish we could have a fine dinner to eat this very minute!' said Skippy at once – and lo and behold, in front of them, on Tickler's round table, appeared a most delicious dinner! A roast chicken sent its tasty smell into the air, and a meat pie stood ready to be served. A large treacle pudding appeared and a plate of big jam tarts.

'Ooh my !' said Tickler, half frightened.

'Let's eat,' said Skippy. So they began to eat, and didn't they enjoy their dinner!

'I'm just going to get some water to drink,' said Skippy, and he hopped off his seat to go to the tap. His shoelace had come undone again, and he fell down on the floor!

'Bother!' he said. 'That shoelace is always tripping me up!'

He did it up and got his water, which he immediately wished into lemonade. Really, it was marvellous!

'Now I shall wish myself a little white pony to ride,' said Skippy. 'And I'll wish you one too, Tickler.'

'I'd rather have a pink pony,' said Tickler. 'That would be most unusual.'

'A pink one wouldn't be nice,' said Skippy, frowning. 'It would look silly. I'll get you a nice white one.'

'I'd rather have a pink one,' said Tickler.

'But *I* shouldn't like a pink pony,' said Skippy.

'Well, it's not you who is to have it, it's me,' said Tickler. 'Wish me a pink one, Skippy.'

'I wish for two nice white ponies,' said Skippy firmly.

At once two little ponies appeared outside in the garden, as white as snow. Skippy got up to run out and nearly tripped over again. His lace was undone.

'Oh, there's that stupid lace undone again!' he cried. He did it up and went outside. 'Come on, Tickler,' he called, 'here's your pony waiting for you. Come and have a ride.'

'I wanted a pink pony,' said Tickler sulkily. 'I don't want a white one.'

'You horrid, ungrateful thing!' cried Skippy. 'Here I've got you a golden suit and a fine meal, and a lovely pony too, and all you can do is to frown at me and look sulky.'

'Well, I wanted a pink pony,' said Tickler. 'A pink pony is uncommon. You were too selfish to let me have what I wanted.'

'I'm *not* selfish!' cried Skippy, in a rage. 'Aren't I sharing all my wishes with you, now? What more do you want?'

'I just want a pink pony,' said Tickler, in an obstinate voice.

'Oh well, have a hundred pink ponies then!' shouted Skippy in a temper – and hey presto, the little garden was at once full to overflowing with small, bright pink ponies!

'Oh, they're treading on my flowers and on my lovely new peas!' shrieked Tickler in dismay. 'Oh, take your horrid ponies away, Skippy!'

'They're not mine, they're yours!' said Skippy dancing about in glee. 'You wanted pink and you've got pink!'

He suddenly tripped headlong over his shoe-lace, which had come undone once more. Down he went, with his nose in the dust.

'Ha, ha, ha! ho, ho!' laughed Tickler. 'That's what comes of being too proud, Skippy. Pride goes before a fall! That shoelace of yours punished you nicely!'

Skippy sat up and looked angrily at his shoe. Yes, that horrid, stupid shoelace was undone again!

'I wish to goodness I'd never put you into my shoe!' said Skippy, crossly, putting out his hand to take the lace to tie again. But it wriggled out of his fingers like a green snake and vanished down the garden path!

And at the same moment all the ponies vanished too! The little white kitten, which had been wandering happily about, suddenly shot up into the air and disappeared like a white cloud.

'Where have all the ponies gone?' said Tickler

in wonder. 'And oh, Skippy, where has your gold suit gone? You've got your old one on again.'

'So have you!' cried Skippy. 'Did you see my shoelace slide off like a snake, Tickler? Wasn't that strange?'

'Where did you get it from?' asked Tickler, suddenly.

'I picked it up in the road,' said Skippy. 'Ooh, Tickler! That's what brought the magic! Of course! When I wished a wish the shoelace always came undone. I remember now – and oh, oh, what a terrible pity, I've wished it away! I've wished my wonderful good luck away!'

'If we hadn't quarrelled it wouldn't have happened,' said Tickler, tears coming into his eyes. 'Oh, Skippy, how foolish we've been. To think we had riches, happiness, everything just for the wishing – and we quarrelled about a pink pony!'

'It shows we weren't big enough to have such a wonderful power,' said Skippy. 'Oh my, oh my, if ever I get a magic shoelace again, won't I just be careful with it!'

But the pity of it was that he never *did* find one again. Do be careful if *you* find one, won't you!

That Little Red Imp

Once upon a time, many years ago, there lived a brownie called Mingy. That wasn't his real name, but he was such a mingy, miserly, mean old fellow that everyone forgot his real name and called him Mingy.

One day he picked up an old kettle from a ditch and looked at it. Yes – if he took it home he could mend that little hole in the bottom and use it. That would save him buying a new kettle!

So he took it home – but, you know, he hadn't looked inside that kettle. If he had, he would have seen that a little red, spidery imp had made it his home, and was very much annoyed at having his kettle taken up from the ditch.

The imp lifted up the lid and took a look at the brownie. He grinned. 'It's old Mingy!' he said to himself. 'I might have guessed. Ho ho! He'll find this kettle a pretty expensive one, before he's done, I think!'

Mingy took the kettle home, mended the hole

and put it up on a shelf to dry. As he turned to sit down there came a knock at the door, and a small elf popped her head in.

'Could you lend me yesterday's newspaper?' she asked. 'I just wanted to see the answer to a puzzle.'

'No, I can't lend it to you,' snapped the brownie, who hated lending even a pin to anyone.

'Mingy, Mingy! Stingy old Mingy!' yelled the little red imp loudly from the kettle.

The brownie looked round, astonished. The imp popped up the kettle lid and grinned at him. 'Mingy, stingy Mingy!' he yelled, in his little high voice.

'Oh, so it's you, is it!' said Mingy, fiercely. 'I'll soon settle *you*!'

The red imp popped out of the kettle and danced up to a higher shelf where some pots of plum jam stood. 'Mingy old stingy! Stingy old Mingy!' he called.

Mingy picked up a duster and flapped hard at the imp. Crash! Smash! Down to the floor came two pots of plum jam and splashed the brownie from head to feet in dark red.

'What a waste, what a waste, Mingy dear!' shouted the red imp. The brownie wiped himself down, in a furious temper. Then he picked up a broom and hit out at the red imp, who had hopped on to the dresser.

The imp took a flying leap on to a shelf full of saucepans and the broom hit a big dish and two glasses. Blim-blam, crash! Down they all came in smithereens, and the red imp jigged about for joy among the saucepans, jumping into first one and then another.

'Mingy, Mingy, isn't he stingy!' he shouted, in his naughty little high voice. The brownie threw the broom at him in a rage, and half the saucepans bounced off the shelf and fell clanging and clanking to the floor, denting themselves terribly.

The red imp hopped back into the kettle, shaking with laughter. Ho ho, old Mingy had got to spend some money now. He must buy new saucepans, a new dish, new glasses!

Mingy suddenly took hold of the kettle and opened the lid. The red imp slipped up the spout and out in a flash. He jumped on to the brownie's shoulder and nipped his ear.

'Mingy, here I am!' he yelled. Mingy put up his hand and tried to slap him, but the imp jumped to the table, where Mingy's tea was set out. The brownie grabbed at him and upset the teapot. The tea went soaking into the tablecloth and into the plate of bread-and-butter.

The red imp jumped into the warm teapot and out again. He *was* enjoying himself. Then he jumped on to the milk jug. Mingy hit out at him – and over went the milk!

Mingy burst into tears. It was too bad! Nasty little imp! Why couldn't he leave him alone?

'Will you go away if I throw the kettle back into the ditch again?' he begged the imp at last. But the red imp shook his head firmly.

'No, certainly not. It's fun living with a stingy old miser like you,' said the imp. 'It's fun to make you break things and spill them, to make you spend your money! Ho ho, I like living with a mingy miser!'

Mingy glared at the imp in rage. Then he put on his hat and went to visit the wise woman next door. He told her his trouble and asked her how he could get rid of the mischievous imp.

'If it's a red imp,' said the wise woman, 'he will love to live with you, Mingy, because red imps love to tease mean, selfish people like you. There's only *one* way of getting rid of him!'

'What's that?' asked Mingy, eagerly.

'Stop being mean and miserly,' said the wise woman, looking over her spectacles at Mingy. 'Then he won't be able to call you names or tease you. It serves you right to be plagued with a nasty little imp like that, Mingy, you know –

you really are rather a nasty little creature yourself!'

Mingy blushed as red as a tomato. How dreadful to have such a thing said to him by a wise woman! He went home hanging his head, and on the way he gave two elves a penny each – a thing he had never in his life done before!

He crept quietly into his cottage – but the red imp was waiting for him.

'Ho ho, here's dear old mingy, old stingy mingy!' he cried, peeping out of the kettle. 'Welcome home, Mingy.'

Mingy said nothing. He hunted about for yesterday's paper and then went out to give it to the little elf who had asked for it. The imp watched him in surprise. When Mingy came back the imp was fast shut in his kettle and didn't even peep out. Mingy was glad.

Tiptap the goblin came knocking at the door that evening and asked Mingy to lend him a little tea. Without a word the brownie opened his tea-caddy and gave Tiptap what he wanted. Tiptap was so astonished that he couldn't say a word. He had never in his life known Mingy to give or lend anything before.

The word soon went round that Mingy was changing. How strange! People said he had a little red imp there too, that sometimes called him names. Stranger still! More and more people called at Mingy's in the next few days to borrow something or to ask for something. Mingy gave them all what they wanted, with a pleasant smile.

A peculiar thing began to happen to him. He felt nice and warm inside whenever he did something kind. He liked the grateful look in people's eyes. He liked their warm smiles at him. It was good to be kind! It was nice to be friendly!

The little red imp had a bad time. It was no good his peeping out of the kettle – no good even to call something rude for Mingy didn't seem to mind.

One day he climbed right out of the kettle and had a good look into Mingy's face.

'Why, I thought you were mean and selfish!' said the red imp. 'I've made a mistake! You are kind! You are good! You're no use to me! I want someone to plague and tease. I want someone to be rude to. Bah! It's no good staying here!'

'Not a bit of good, imp,' said Mingy. 'I'll put your kettle back in the ditch, if you like.'

The imp climbed into his kettle and the brownie threw it into the ditch where he had found it.

'That's the end of *you*!' he thought with glee.

'Now, if I want to, I can go back to my old ways!'

But the strange thing was that he *didn't* want to! There was no fun in being mean! He didn't feel warm and happy when he was being selfish! No, he wanted to smile, and to see others smile. He wanted to be generous and get that nice warm feeling inside. It was much more fun to be kind!

So the little red imp was some good after all! He is still living in his old kettle down in the ditch. You may find him there one day, if you look – but first be sure you're not a mingy fellow yourself, or I shall be very sorry for you!

The Little Fat Dormouse

There was once a fat dormouse who lived in a cosy home in the hedge with his mother and father and four brothers and sisters. His name was Pitterpat because his feet went pitter-pattering like rain along the bank by his home.

Pitterpat didn't like being a dormouse. He was small, too small, he thought. Why couldn't he be big, like a rabbit, or have sharp claws, like a cat? Then he would be Somebody!

He thought he was much cleverer than his family. He was always laughing at them and telling them they were stupid. At last his brothers and sisters turned him out of the nest, and said:

'If you are so clever, go and find another home! Let us know when you have made your fortune and we will come and admire you – but until you have done something great, leave us to ourselves!'

Pitterpat was very angry. He picked up his little bag and set off, vowing to himself that he would soon show his brothers and sisters what a clever fellow he was. Ha, he would be a cow, or a horse, or even a sharp weasel if he could find one who would teach him all the tricks.

Soon he came to a field. In it there were some sheep grazing, and Pitterpat went up to one of them.

'Madam,' he said, politely. 'I am a clever dormouse, but I would like to be a sheep. Will you tell me how?'

'Certainly,' said the surprised sheep, looking at the tiny dormouse. 'Can you baa?'

Pitterpat tried. He could squeak, but he could not seem to baa.

'Well, never mind,' said the sheep. 'You must grow wool on your back.'

'But that would be so hot,' said the dormouse. 'It is summertime.'

'You *must* grow wool if you want to be like us,' said the sheep.

'I don't think I will be a sheep,' said the dormouse and he scurried away, thinking that sheep must be stupid to wear wool in the summer. Soon he came to where a rabbit nibbled grass outside its hole.

'Sir,' he said, 'I am a clever dormouse, but I would like to be a rabbit. Will you tell me how?'

'Well, you must learn to make a great home of

burrows under the ground,' said the rabbit. 'You must use your paws like this to scrape up the earth.' The rabbit scraped a shower of earth up and it fell all over the dormouse.

'That's a stupid thing to do,' said the dormouse, angrily. 'Look how dirty you have made me.'

The rabbit took no notice. 'Then,' he went on, 'you must grow a short, fluffy white bobtail like mine. It acts as a danger-signal to everyone when I run to my hole. My friends see my bobbing tail and run too.'

'My tail is much better than yours,' said the dormouse scornfully. 'I don't think I will be a rabbit.' He ran away, thinking what a stupid creature the rabbit was, covering him with earth like that and talking about bobtails.

He came to a pond after a while and saw a fine white duck squatting beside the water, basking in the sun. He went up and bowed.

'Madam!' he said. 'I am a clever dormouse, but I would like to be a duck. Will you tell me how?'

'First you must quack like this,' said the duck, and she opened her beak and quacked so loudly that the dormouse was half frightened. He opened his mouth and tried to quack too, but all the sound he made was a small squeal.

'And then,' said the duck, 'you must swim, like this!' She flopped into the water, and it splashed all over the watching dormouse, soaking him to the skin.

'You silly, stupid duck, look what you've done!' he cried in anger. 'You've nearly drowned me.'

'Oh, you'll have to get used to a wetting if you're going to be a duck,' quacked the duck, merrily.

'I don't think I will be a duck!' called the dormouse and hurried away. 'Silly creature,' he thought. 'Splashing me like that!'

A grunting noise made him stop. He looked under a gate and saw a large, fat pig in a sty. Ah, how big and fine he looked! The dormouse crept under the gate and spoke to the pig.

'Sir,' he said, 'I am a clever dormouse, but I would like to be a pig. Will you tell me how?'

'Can you grunt, like this?' said the surprised pig and grunted in such a vulgar manner that the dormouse was quite disgusted.

'I shouldn't wish to make such a rude noise as that,' he said, his nose in the air. The pig grunted again and began to root about in the mud of his sty so roughly that poor Pitterpat was sent head-over-heels into a dirty puddle.

'You must learn to root about like this,' said

the pig, twinkling his little eyes cheekily at the dormouse. 'Oh, did I upset you?'

The dormouse picked himself up out of the mud and looked angrily at the pig.

'I don't think I will be a pig,' he said, huffily. 'Nasty, dirty, ill-mannered creatures!'

The pig laughed gruntily, and the dormouse pattered off. Ugh! He wouldn't be a dirty old pig for anything!

Outside the farmyard he met a sharp-nosed rat. This rat was eating potato parings which he had pulled from the rubbish-heap. The dormouse watched the rat, and noticed his clever, sharp eyes and the way in which he held the food in his front paws. Ah, here was a clever fellow, to be sure! Not stupid like the rabbit and sheep, not wicked like the duck, not dirty like the pig. He would be a rat!

'Sir,' said the dormouse, going nearer. 'I am a clever dormouse, but I would like to be a rat. Will you tell me how?'

'Certainly,' said the rat. 'Can you squeal like this?' He squealed shrilly. The dormouse opened his mouth and squealed too.

'Not so bad,' said the rat. 'Now can you hold food in your paws as I do?' The dormouse tried, and found he could do it easily. He was delighted. Ah yes, he would certainly be a rat!

'What else must I do?' he asked.

'You must learn to pounce on your victims like this,' said the rat, and he leapt to one side. 'See, this is how I catch a young bird! And see, this is how I pounce on a frog! And SEE! This is how I pounce on silly little dormice!'

He leapt at the astonished dormouse – but Pitterpat gave a frightened squeal and fled for his life. Down a molehole he went and into a maze of small tunnels. The rat followed him, hungry for a dinner.

The dormouse slipped aside into a tiny hole he knew of, hoping that the rat would pass before he guessed he was there. The rat did pass – and at once Pitterpat turned and fled back the way he had come, never stopping once until he had got back to his own cosy home again, high up in the hedgerow.

As he scrambled into the big, round nest all his sisters and brothers cried out in surprise. 'Oh, here's the clever one back again! Have you made your fortune?'

'No,' said the dormouse, hanging his head. 'I haven't made a fortune but I've made a lot of mistakes. I'm not clever, I'm very stupid. Forgive me and let me live here again with you.'

So his family forgave him, and the little dormouse lived happily in the hedgerow. 'It's best to be what you are!' he thought. 'I'm *glad* I'm a stupid little dormouse!'

The Greedy Toy Clown

Once there was a toy clown. He lived in the nursery cupboard with all the other toys, but nobody liked him very much. For one thing he was very thin, and for another he was greedy.

If ever the toys had a tea party he was sure to eat most of the cakes, and once he even put some sandwiches in his pocket when he thought no one was looking. He meant to eat them all by himself in the night.

He was very proud of his blue trousers and red coat, and proudest of all of a lovely glittering brooch that Ann had given him out of a Christmas cracker. Ann was the little girl the toys belonged to. They liked her very much because she played every day with them, and was gentle and kind.

One day Ann had a lovely present given to her. It was a proper little stove! It had an oven inside and saucepans and kettles on top. You could really light it and cook with it. Ann loved it and cooked little puddings for herself of biscuits and sugar.

Now when everything was dark and still one night, the clown awoke and stretched himself. He was hungry. He remembered the little stove. What fun if he could creep out and cook himself a meal on it! None of the other toys were about. Ann had been playing with them such a lot that day that they were all feeling too tired to stir out of the cupboard.

So the clown tiptoed out alone. He went to the little gas stove and looked at it. How lovely it was! He was sure he could cook with it. But what could he cook?

He looked around. He couldn't really see anything to cook for his supper – and then he suddenly saw the little toy sweet shop that Ann had. There were little bottles of sweets in it, and packets of chocolate and lozenges. He would take some of those and cook them.

So he went to the shop, opened the door and went behind the counter. Wasn't it naughty of him? He took some sweets out of a bottle, a packet of chocolate and shook some lozenges into his hand. What a fine meal he would cook with all those mixed in a saucepan together!

He tiptoed back to the stove and emptied the sweets into a saucepan. He took it to the doll's house, turned on the bathroom tap there and half-filled the saucepan with water. That was to cook the sweets in. He thought it would make a lovely sweet-pudding!

Then he found some matches in a box by the fireplace and lit the stove. The flame shot up, and he put the saucepan over it. Now his dinner would cook!

The clown was pleased with himself. Ha, he would have a fine meal while all the other toys were asleep. The saucepan was nearly boiling, his supper would soon be ready. How good it smelt!

He did a little dance round the stove – and then a dreadful thing happened His sleeve caught the handle of the saucepan and over it went!

Splish-splash! The boiling water shot out and some of it fell on the clown's legs. Goodness, how he squealed!

His shrieks woke up all the other toys, of course. They came pouring out of the cupboard wondering whatever the matter was. When they saw the clown holding his leg, and discovered the spilt saucepan, with all the sticky mess on the carpet, they guessed what he had been doing!

'It serves you right!' said the teddy bear. 'You're far too sly and greedy. How dare you take sweets from the shop and use Ann's stove?

Stop making that noise. Go and get some vaseline out of the box on the shelf and tie up your leg with your handkerchief. If you've scalded it, it is a good punishment for you!'

The clown hopped off, crying. The wooden doll tried to scrape up the hot, sticky mess from the nursery carpet – and, oh dear me, it came away with a bit of the carpet and left a hole there!

The toys stared at it in dismay. Whatever could be done about that? Ann would see it, and perhaps Ann would be scolded for something she hadn't done! It must be mended *some*how.

'What shall we do?' asked the teddy bear, quite upset.

'We'd better ask the elf who lives in the lavender bed outside if she'll come and mend the hole,' said the clockwork duck. 'I sometimes see her when Ann takes me down the path, and she's always sewing, so I expect she could easily mend that hole.'

'Good idea!' said the bear. So he went to the window and called the elf softly. She soon came – and when she heard what they wanted her to do, she went back to get her needle and threads. She sat down on the carpet and began to sew. All the toys watched her. You wouldn't believe how beautifully she did it! Her threads were fine but strong, and she matched up the carpet perfectly.

'There!' she said, when it was done. 'Is that all right?'

'It's beautiful!' cried all the toys. 'What would you like for a reward?'

'I should love a little brooch,' said the elf, shyly. 'I haven't one, you know.'

'Clown! Give the elf your glittering brooch!' said the teddy bear, at once, beckoning the clown forward.

'But I don't want to,' he said. 'I like it.'

'That doesn't matter,' said the wooden doll. 'You caused damage by your greediness, and so you must suffer for it. The elf has put things right and you must reward her. Give her your brooch, quickly!'

The clown undid it, with tears in his eyes. The elf took it gladly and pinned it at her neck. It looked fine! She was most delighted.

'Goodbye!' she said. 'I hope nobody will ever notice the mend.' Nobody did – but Ann soon saw that the clown had lost his brooch. She hunted for it everywhere, but of course she never found it. As for the clown, he isn't vain or greedy any more. Fancy that!

Timothy Toad

One morning when Janet was riding down the lane on her bicycle she saw something crawling in the road. She got off her bicycle and went to see what it was – and she saw that it was a big toad, whose hind foot had been squashed by a passing car.

Janet looked at the hurt toad and the toad looked back. He had the loveliest coppery eyes, like jewels, and as Janet looked at him he put up his front hand and rubbed his nose.

'You seem quite tame!' said Janet, who wasn't altogether sure that she liked toads. She looked at him again, and really, it did seem as if he were just about to speak to her. But he didn't, of course. He gave a deep croak and tried to crawl away again, dragging his leg behind him.

'You'll get run over by a car,' said Janet. 'You shouldn't walk in the road. Your poor leg is already squashed by something.'

The little girl didn't like to leave the toad there. She felt sure he would be run over. So she took her handkerchief out of her pocket, wrapped the toad up in it and carefully put it on the side of the road.

The toad stretched out its leg as if to show her that it was hurt. Janet, who was a very kind-hearted child, wondered if she ought to do something for its leg. So she picked it up in her handkerchief and carried it home. Her daddy was working in the garden and called out to find out what she had.

'A hurt toad!' said Janet.

'Let's see,' said Daddy. So the little girl showed him.

'Dear, dear!' said Daddy. 'He *has* hurt his foot, hasn't he! Let's put some ointment on it. That will help it to get better.'

So they doctored the toad's foot. He was very good. He sat on Daddy's hand, looking up with his fine, copper eyes, and then, when they had finished with him he crawled away into the flower bed.

'Will he eat the flowers, Daddy?' asked Janet. 'The tortoise ate our violas, you know.'

'No, he won't touch the plants,' said Daddy. 'He likes an insect dinner!'

Janet looked for the toad the next day, but she couldn't find him. He seemed to be gone. She wondered if his foot was better, and was glad that she had brought him home so that Daddy could see to him.

Daddy was always gardening. He grew such a lot of flowers and vegetables. The broad beans were full of fine pods. The early peas were flowering. The gooseberries were ripe enough to pick. Daddy was very pleased with his garden – except for just one thing.

And that was his lettuces! He had planted out a long row of small plants – and then two days later nearly all of them had gone! Daddy *was* upset.

'The slugs have had them,' he told Janet. 'They really are a pest this year. You might help me this evening, Janet. We'll hunt for them and catch as many as we can. Then I'll plant out another row of lettuces.'

So Janet and Daddy hunted for slugs, and they found a great many. The next day Daddy planted out another row of lettuces – nice little plants with two or three leaves each.

'In a few weeks' time they will be fine big lettuces,' said Daddy. 'Then we can take them in for tea. They will be lovely with new bread-and-butter!'

For a few days the lettuces grew well – and then came a wet day and night. In the night the slugs crept out again from the hiding places under the stone edgings and beneath the pebbles on the bed – and how they feasted on those lettuces!

Really, when Daddy and Janet came to look at them the next day they could hardly believe their eyes! Only about nine miserable little half-eaten plants remained. It was too bad.

'Well, I shall only try once again,' said Daddy. 'I've enough plants for one more time. If the slugs get at those I shall have to give up.'

So once more he and Janet planted them out in neat rows. They sprinkled soot round them to keep off the slugs, but when the rain came it washed the soot all away!

'I don't expect these will escape the slugs,' said Daddy.

But, you know, they did! Day after day Daddy and Janet went to look at the lettuces, expecting to see them eaten up. But not a single lettuce died. All of them shot up strong and green and began to make fine plants.

'It's strange,' said Daddy, in surprise, looking in vain for slugs. 'I wonder where all those slugs have gone to.'

'Oh, Daddy, look!' cried Janet, suddenly. She pointed to a big lettuce – and what do you think was behind it? A great fat toad! As Daddy and Janet looked at him he shot out his tongue and caught a big blue-bottle fly that was sitting on a nearby leaf.

'Why, Janet, there's the fellow who's got rid of all those slugs for us!' said Daddy. 'A toad is a good friend in the garden – he eats all kinds of insects, and loves a meal of slugs. He has certainly saved our lettuces for us.'

Janet bent down to look at him. He stared up at her, his bright eyes gleaming.

'Do you know, Daddy,' said Janet, excited. 'It's the toad whose foot was hurt! Look, it's better now, but you can see where it was hurt. Oh, Daddy! Just think! We were friends to him and now he's a friend to us! He's saved our lettuces. Do you suppose he knew?'

'I can't tell,' said Daddy, 'but I shouldn't be surprised. You never know what a minute's kindness will bring you in return! Good old toad, we'll call you Timothy, and you shall live in our garden all your life!'

He's still there, because I've seen him!

Brer Rabbit Gets in a Fix

Once it happened that Brer Fox found Brer Rabbit fishing in his favourite fishing-place, and he was so angry that he pounced on Brer Rabbit and nearly caught him. But Brer Rabbit was just a little bit too quick, and he got away, leaving a tuft of his fur in Brer Fox's claws.

Brer Fox was so excited to think how nearly he had caught Brer Rabbit that he raced after him at top speed. Brer Fox could go as fast as a race-horse when he liked, and he meant to catch Brer Rabbit this time.

There were no rabbit-holes near the fishing-place, and Brer Rabbit was in a bad way, for there was nowhere he could hide. He just ran on and on, lippitty-clippitty, hoping to find a thick bush or hole.

But there was nothing at all, and Brer Fox was getting nearer and nearer. At last Brer Rabbit spied Brer Wolf's house in the distance, and he ran up to it. He leapt up the gutter-pipe by the side of the house and sat on the roof. Brer

Fox stopped and looked up. The gutter-pipe wouldn't bear his weight – he could see that – but all the same he had got Brer Rabbit very nicely caught! A ladder would get him down all right, and then he would pop him into a pan and stew him for dinner. Oho!

Brer Wolf came out to see what all the noise was about, and he was mighty astonished to see Brer Rabbit sitting up on his roof, panting and puffing, and Brer Fox down below, snarling in delight.

'I've got old Brer Rabbit at last!' said Brer Fox. 'Have you a pan big enough to stew him in, Brer Wolf?'

'No, I haven't,' said Brer Wolf. 'He looks pretty fat to me. He'll need a bigger pan than *I* have.'

'Well, will you just keep watch on him to see he doesn't escape,' said Brer Fox, 'and I'll go and get my biggest pan.'

Off went Brer Fox at a run and Brer Wolf sat down in his garden, his gleaming eyes fixed on Brer Rabbit. But Brer Rabbit didn't seem at all worried. He just sat up on the roof and washed his ears for a little while, and then he began to sniff about round the chimney nearby. Presently Brer Wolf heard him scraping at a tile, and pretty soon it came loose.

'Hey, Brer Rabbit, what are you doing?' shouted Brer Wolf. 'You leave my roof alone.'

'All right, all right, Brer Wolf,' said Brer Rabbit. 'I just thought there was something under this tile, that's all.'

'What do you mean, something under the tile?' asked Brer Wolf.

'Oh, just something,' answered Brer Rabbit, scraping the tile back into place. Just then something fell down the roof and bounced near Brer Wolf. It was a piece of money! Brer Wolf pounced on it and looked at it in surprise.

'What was that?' asked Brer Rabbit, peering over the edge of the roof.

'It's a piece of money!' cried Brer Wolf. 'My, Brer Rabbit, it must have come from under that tile!'

'Or it might have dropped out of my pocket,' said Brer Rabbit. 'You throw it back to me, Brer Wolf.'

'Ho, ho, you think you'll rob me of secret money hidden under my roof, do you?' said Brer Wolf. 'No, I'm not so stupid as that, Brer Rabbit. I'm going to get a ladder and come up there to see what's hidden under that loose tile by the chimney. Whatever's there is mine, because the roof is mine!'

Brer Wolf took up his ladder, which was

nearby and leaned it against the roof. He climbed up and was soon sitting beside Brer Rabbit.

'Now, where's that tile?' he asked him.

'It's just here, by the chimney,' said Brer Rabbit, and he showed Brer Wolf the tile he had moved. 'Hold on to the chimney, Brer Wolf, and you can scrape away the tile with your other hand.'

Brer Wolf held on tightly to the chimney, and began to scratch away at the tile. It was hard to move and he pushed away, quite forgetting all about Brer Rabbit. Brer Rabbit slid down to the edge of the roof, got on to the ladder, and was down it in a twink! He made his way to a bramble-bush, where he knew there was a hole, and there he sat, his whiskers shaking with delight.

Brer Wolf went on scratching and scraping at the tile, and didn't hear Brer Fox coming back. Brer Fox came along dragging a great pan by the handle, and he was most astonished to see Brer Wolf up on the roof and no Brer Rabbit anywhere.

'Heyo, Brer Wolf!' he shouted. 'Where's Brer Rabbit?'

Brer Wolf almost fell off the roof in horror when he saw Brer Rabbit was gone, and Brer

Fox down below looking mighty angry.

'Has Brer Rabbit gone?' he said at last.

Brer Fox nearly had a fit. When he could speak he almost choked with rage. 'Do you mean to tell me that you let Brer Rabbit go when you knew I'd gone to fetch a pan to stew him in?' he shouted. 'And anyway what are *you* doing up on the roof, Brer Wolf, scratching away like mad?'

'Oh, I think there's a fortune hidden somewhere about this chimney,' said Brer Wolf. 'Brer Rabbit got this tile loose and a piece of money fell down to the ground. Come on up, Brer Fox, and don't look so angry down there. If we can find a fortune what does it matter about losing a skinny creature like Brer Rabbit.'

'He wasn't skinny,' said Brer Fox, climbing up the ladder. 'Well, Brer Wolf, if you'll share your good fortune with me, I'll say no more about you letting Brer Rabbit go.'

Soon the tile came loose and fell to the ground and smashed. The two on the roof put their paws down to find the hidden gold they expected – but there was none there! No, not a single piece of money was to be found!

'Brer Rabbit's been telling you stories!' cried Brer Fox, in a rage. 'There's nothing there!'

'I've been telling *no* stories!' said Brer

Rabbit's voice from the garden. 'Didn't I say, Brer Wolf, that that piece of money must have fallen out of my pocket? Well, it did!'

Brer Wolf and Brer Fox glared at Brer Rabbit in a fury – and as they sat up there, glaring, Brer Rabbit kicked the ladder so that it fell flat on the ground.

'You'd better stay up on the roof a bit longer,' he grinned. 'I'm not going to be chased home by two great bullies like you! I'm going home slowly. Goodbye, Brer Fox! Goodbye, Brer Wolf!'

And with that off went Brer Rabbit, sauntering along as if he had all the day before him to get home. As for Brer Fox and Brer Wolf, there they had to stay, up on the roof, and it was a mighty long time before they managed to get down!

The Skippetty Shoes

Mr Winkle was a shoemaker. He lived in a tiny, tumbledown cottage, and all day long he sat outside on a bench and made or mended shoes. He was a merry, mischievous fellow, always ready for a joke. Sometimes he played naughty tricks and made his friends cross.

One time he ran a glue brush inside a pair of shoes that he sold to Father Grumps – and dear me, how Grumps tugged and pulled to get those shoes from his feet! In the end both his socks came too, and Father Grumps was very angry indeed.

Another time Winkle put a squeak into the heels of some boots he sold to Dame Twisty, and when she heard the squeak-squeak-squeak as she walked, she really thought it was a goblin coming after her, and she fled down the street in fright, her shoes squeaking loudly all the time! Yes, really, Mr Winkle was a mischievous fellow.

He got worse as he grew older, instead of

better, People shook their heads and said: 'One day he will go too far, and then who knows what will happen to him?'

Now, one morning, as Mr Winkle sat mending shoes, and humming a little song that went 'Tol-de-ray, shoes for a fay, tol-de-rome, shoes for a gnome,' a fat gnome came by. He stood and watched Winkle at work, and Winkle looked up and grinned.

'You've a lot of time to waste!' he said, cheekily.

The gnome frowned. He felt in his bag and brought out a pair of old slippers, each of which had a hole in the sole. They had once been grand slippers, for there was a gold buckle on each, and the heels were made of silver.

'How long will you take to mend these?' asked the gnome.

'One hour,' answered Winkle, looking at them. 'My, how grand they were once – but they are very old now, and hardly worth mending.'

'They are most comfortable slippers,' said the gnome, 'and that is why they are to be mended, Mr Winkle. Now, set to work, and keep your tongue still. It wags all day long.'

'Better than growling all day long, like yours!' answered Winkle, cheekily. The gnome frowned again, and sat himself down on a stool.

Winkle tried to make him talk, but he wouldn't say a word. He just sat there and thought.

Mr Winkle felt annoyed. What an old solemn-face the gnome was! Cross old stick, thought Winkle, as he began to mend the slippers. His needle flew in and out, and his busy little brain thought about the old fat gnome.

Presently an idea came into his naughty mind. He would play a trick on the gnome. But what trick could he play? He thought and thought – and then he got up and went indoors. Somewhere he had got a little Skippetty Spell – but where was it? If only he could find it, what a fine trick he would play on the old fat gnome!

He hunted here and he hunted there – and at last he found it, tucked inside a milk jug. Good! Winkle hurried back to his bench, and found the gnome looking crossly at him.

'Where have you been?' he said. 'Get on with your work. I want those shoes finished at once.'

Winkle made a face and sewed quickly at the shoes. Into each he sewed half of the Skippetty Spell, grinning to himself as he thought of how the gnome would kick, jump, leap and prance, as soon as he put those slippers on his feet. Ho, ho! That would be a funny sight to watch! That would teach the solemn old fellow to frown at him and talk crossly!

'The slippers are finished,' said Winkle at last. He handed them to the gnome, and took his payment. But still the old fellow sat there on his stool, as if he were waiting for someone.

'What are you waiting for?' asked Winkle.

'The king is coming to call for me here,' said the gnome. 'He said he would fetch me in his carriage. It is his shoes you have mended. They are his oldest ones, but so comfortable that he cannot bear to get new ones.'

Winkle stared in horror. Gracious goodness, were they really the king's own slippers? He was just going to take them from the gnome when there came the sound of galloping hooves, and up came the king's carriage. The gnome stood up and went to the gate. The carriage stopped and the king leaned out.

'Did you get my shoes mended?' he asked.

'Yes, Your Majesty,' said the gnome and gave them to the king. His Majesty kicked off his grand gold boots and slipped his feet contentedly into his old slippers.

'Oh, how nice to have these again!' he began – and then he stopped in dismay. Oh, those slippers! As soon as they were on the king's feet the Skippetty Spell began to work, and what a shock they gave His Majesty!

They jumped him out of the carriage. They

made him kick his legs up into the air. His crown fell off into a lavender bush, and his cloak was shaken all crooked. He pranced round the garden, he kicked high, he kicked low, he jumped over the wall, and he spun round and round till he was quite giddy. Certainly that Skippetty Spell was very powerful indeed!

The gnome stared at the king in horror. Mr Winkle turned pale and trembled. When the gnome saw Winkle's face he knew that he must have played a trick. He was full of rage and he caught the trembling cobbler by the collar.

'What have you done to the king's slippers, you wicked creature?' he shouted.

'There's a Sk-Skippetty Sp-Spell in them,' stammered Winkle. 'Do you know how to get it out? I don't!'

Luckily the old gnome was a clever fellow, and he knew how to deal with a Skippetty Spell. He clapped his hands seven times, called out a strange magic word, and hey presto the spell flew out of the slippers, they stopped dancing, and the king sat down to get his breath.

Mr Winkle knelt down and begged the king's pardon – but he was far too angry to listen.

'Take your tools and go away from Fairy-land!' roared the king. 'I've a good mind to turn you into an earwig, you mischievous little creature! Go away before I think of the right word!'

Winkle was in a terrible fright. He was so afraid of turning into an earwig that he caught up his bag of tools then and there and fled right away. He ran until he came to the borders of Fairyland, and not till then did he feel safe. He kept looking at himself, to see if he were Winkle, or an earwig.

Now he lives in our world. He still makes shoes for the pixies – very tiny ones, gold and black. He has no shop now, so he has to store them somewhere else – and do you know where he puts them? I'll tell you.

Find a white dead-nettle blossom and lift up the flower so that you can peep inside the top lip. What do you see there? Yes – two pairs of tiny pixie slippers, hung up safely by Mr Winkle the cobbler! Aren't they sweet? Don't forget to go and look for them, will you?

Jerry's Lost Temper

Once upon a time there lived a little boy who was always losing his temper. He lost it about six times a day, and that made him most unpleasant to live with.

He lost his temper at breakfast time when his mother made him eat his porridge, and threw his spoon at her. He lost it in the middle of the morning when his spade broke. He lost it at dinner time when he wanted a third helping of jelly and there wasn't any. He lost it twice at tea time because his mother wanted him to finish up his bread-and-butter, and he lost it when he was in the bath, because his duck wouldn't float properly.

So you can see what a bad-tempered child he was! It was really dreadful to see him and hear him.

'One of these days, Jerry,' said his mother, 'you'll lose your temper and not be able to find it again! That will be a great shock to you, because little boys and girls who lose their tempers for always, can never smile or laugh, but can only sulk, frown and cry, and talk in a cross-patch voice! You really should be careful!'

Now, one day, Jerry went to spend the day with his Aunt Marigold, who lived at the very end of Foxglove Village. His mother told him to be sure and behave nicely and to keep his temper, not to lose it.

But he hadn't been at his aunt's for five minutes before he flew into a terrible rage, quite lost his temper, and threw a saucepan lid at the big black cat sitting peacefully by the fire! That was the worst of Jerry. He always threw things when he lost his temper.

The saucepan lid hit the cat on the head. She hissed and jumped aside. Then she turned on the little boy and scratched him hard.

'Oh, dear!' said his aunt. 'Cinders is a queer cat, and whenever he scratches anybody something unpleasant happens. Now, Jerry, don't look so cross. Go out into the garden and don't come in again until you've found that temper you've lost!'

She pushed the angry little boy out of doors, and shut the kitchen door firmly. Jerry wandered round the garden, scowling. Suddenly he heard a call and, looking up, he saw the little girl next door holding out an apple to him.

'Hello, Jerry!' she said. 'Have an apple!'

Jerry tried to smile his thanks – but, to his horror, a smile wouldn't come! Instead a terrible frown puckered up his forehead and his lips pouted into a sulk.

'Oh, all right!' said the little girl, offended at Jerry's black looks. 'If you don't want a nice apple, *I'll* eat it!'

She dug her teeth into it, slid off the wall and disappeared. Jerry was dreadfully disappointed. He wondered what was wrong with his face. No matter how hard he tried to smile, he couldn't make his lips go up – they always went down. And his forehead kept wrinkling into a frown – but, worst of all, when he tried to speak he found that his voice had changed into a fierce growl, like a dog's!

'Oh, goodness gracious!' thought poor Jerry to himself. 'What Mother said would happen has come true! I've really and truly lost my temper this time and it hasn't come back!'

Jerry ran into a corner and cried bitterly. He tried again and again to speak, but he could only growl. He tried to stop frowning but he couldn't. Then he heard his aunt calling him.

'Jerry! Jerry! Here is a piece of chocolate cake for you!'

Jerry loved chocolate cake! He forgot his tears

and ran eagerly to the kitchen door, where his Aunt Marigold stood holding an enormous piece of iced chocolate cake. But, when she saw the scowling, frowning face of the little boy, and heard his growling, angry voice, she stared in surprise.

'What a dreadful, cross face!' she said. 'No, Jerry – you can't have the cake if you look like that!'

She went indoors, and shut the door, taking the cake with her. Jerry banged on the door, trying to say that he didn't mean to look cross and to growl – but his aunt was annoyed with him and wouldn't open the door. So the little boy ran off to the bottom of the garden, more miserable and more frightened than he had ever been in his life before.

What would happen if he never found his temper again, if it was always lost? How people would hate him! He would never get any treats, but would always be left out of everything. Jerry was very, very sad.

'What's the matter?' suddenly asked a high voice just beside him. Jerry looked down and saw a sharp-faced little man looking up at him. He was not a fairy, but looked more like a funny little dwarf.

'I've lost my temper, and I can't find it again,'

said Jerry, in a strange, snarling voice, frowning at the little dwarf.

'Ho, ho!' said the little creature, laughing. 'So that's what's the matter! Well, *I've* got your temper, little boy! I collect bad tempers, when I find them, and sell them to a cross old witch, who lives on the edge of the world. She pays me well for them. I found yours flying round the garden this morning, and I've got it safely in my pocket!'

'Please give it back to me!' begged Jerry, in the same growly voice. 'I can't bear to be like this, all frowns, sulks and snarls! It's horrid!'

'But you're like it a dozen times a day!' said the dwarf, grinning. 'I know you are! I've been close to you for a long time, though you didn't know it – and I knew I should be able to find that bad temper of yours, one day, when you lost it. And now I've got it!'

'Please,' said Jerry, still in his snarly voice. 'Please do give it back to me. I promise you that if I lose it again you may have it for good. I do promise you! But let me have it back again, just this once.'

'Well,' said the little dwarf, putting his hand into his pocket, 'I'm pretty sure you'll lose it again in the next ten minutes, so I don't mind letting you have it. Here you are. Swallow it –

but mind, I shall get it again before very long!'

Jerry took from the dwarf's hand a small, soft, yellow thing, rather the shape of an egg, with bright red ends that gleamed. He popped it into his mouth and swallowed it down – his lost temper!

At once he began to smile, and his own proper voice came back. His terrible frown went, and he looked friendly and pleasant.

'Goodness! That's made a difference to you!' said the dwarf, in surprise. 'Well, well – you'll get your frowns back in a minute or two, I expect, when you lose your temper again. And I shall catch that temper of yours and keep it to sell to the old witch! Ho, ho!'

Jerry said no more to the little dwarf. He ran straight to the kitchen door and opened it.

'Aunt Marigold, Aunt Marigold!' he cried. 'I've come to say I'm sorry I lost my temper this morning, and you may be sure I shall never do such a thing again. Please forgive me!'

And do you know, from that day to this Jerry never *has* lost his temper. He's so afraid the little dwarf will find it and keep it to sell to the witch. I do hope you won't ever lose yours when he's about – wouldn't it be dreadful if he found it and didn't give it back!

Mr Tickles' Green Pen

Once upon a time a brownie called Mr Tickles had a fine green pen. He was very proud of it, for it was a beautiful green, and it wrote very well indeed. It was a fountain pen, and he always kept it full of ink, so that he might write letters at any time.

But he was always losing it! Sometimes it was found on the dresser, sometimes on the mantelpiece, and once in the middle of the best bed, which made Mrs Tickles very angry indeed, for it had left a spot of ink behind.

'Tickles, why can't you keep your green pen in your pocket?' she said, a dozen times a week. 'You are always losing it. You must waste hours and hours trying to find it.'

'I know,' said Tickles. 'It is a great nuisance. I do try to remember to put it into my pocket, but it so often falls out, you know. And besides, I already have two pencils and a notebook in my pocket. There really isn't room for a pen too.'

'Well, why not do as the butcher boy does?' said Mrs Tickles.

'What does he do?' asked Mr Tickles.

'He puts his pen behind his right ear,' said Mrs Tickles. 'He comes every morning to take my order, and he has never to hunt for his pen for there it always is, tucked safely behind his ear!'

'What a splendid idea!' said Mr Tickles. 'I wonder if *my* ear will hold my green pen.'

He hunted about for his pen and found it stuck in a jug on the dresser. He put it behind his right ear and it held it beautifully. He was very pleased.

'Now I shall always know where it is!' he said, rubbing his hands. 'Aha! I shall waste no more time in looking for it again!'

'That's good,' said his wife. 'Now listen, Tickles, I'm going out to do my shopping. Will you please write a note to the sweep while I am gone, and ask him to come and sweep the chimney next Saturday? Now don't forget because it is most important and I shan't have time to do any letter writing today.'

Tickles promised to do the letter, and his wife took her basket and went out. Tickles cleaned his new boots, and then he scraped out his pipe, for it was very dirty. Then he frowned.

'Now, what was it that Mrs Tickles said she wanted me to do?' he wondered. 'Ah, yes – I promised to write a note to the sweep. Well, I'll do it now before I forget!'

He took out his notepaper and sat down. He felt in his pocket for his green pen. But it wasn't there. Bother! Where was it?

'That pen is always disappearing!' grumbled Mr Tickles, crossly. 'Now where did I put it?'

He hunted here and he hunted there. He looked on the dresser, he looked under the table. He went into the bedroom and looked on the bed. He looked simply everywhere! But he couldn't find that green pen.

'Let me see,' said Mr Tickles. 'I cleaned out my pipe this morning and put the scrapings in the dustbin. I believe, yes, I really do believe that my green pen must have dropped into the dustbin. Oh, dear!'

Just then, who should come into the garden but the dustman to take away the rubbish from the dustbin. He picked up the bin and strode out to his cart. Mr Tickles tapped loudly on the window.

'Wait, wait!' he cried. 'There is something valuable in the dustbin!'

But alas! The dustman had already tipped the dustbin into his cart. Mr Tickles ran out and scolded him.

'Why didn't you wait when you heard me

tapping at my window? My green fountain pen, the only one I have, has disappeared, and I'm sure it must have dropped into the dustbin. Now it's gone into the cart.'

'Well, sir,' said the dustman, 'I could go through the rubbish for you, if you like, and find your pen.'

'You'd better do that,' said Mr Tickles. 'I really *must* have my green pen back.'

The dustman began to search through the rubbish. He hunted through the cabbage leaves and the tea leaves, he looked in all the old tins, and he shook out the papers. But he couldn't find that pen anywhere. At last he went back to Mr Tickles.

'I'm very sorry, sir,' he said, 'but I can't find that pen of yours.'

'Dear, dear, how foolish of you!' said Mr Tickles. 'I tell you it *must* be there!'

The dustman took a piece of paper from his pocket and gave it to Mr Tickles. 'If you'll just sign that paper, sir,' he said, 'I'll see that your pen is hunted for once again, when I get back to the works. But I can't stop and look any longer myself, because I'm late as it is.'

'Very well, I'll sign the paper,' said Mr Tickles, impatiently. 'Dear me, I wish I'd looked in the cart myself for my pen – I'm sure I should have found it. It's too bad to lose a fine green pen like that!'

He put the piece of paper on the flat top of his gatepost to sign it. He took his green pen from behind his ear, where he had so carefully put it, and signed his name. The dustman stared at him in amazement.

'Now, what are you staring at me like that for?' asked Mr Tickles, putting back his pen behind his ear. 'Really, really, it is very rude of you!'

'It may be rude,' said the dustman. 'But pray tell me this, Mr Tickles – why do you make me waste my time in looking for your green pen when you have it behind your ear all the time? You have just signed your name with it!'

Mr Tickles put up his hand – and, of course, there was his green pen, behind his ear, just as the dustman had said! He did feel dreadful! He went first pink, then red, then purple.

'How foolish I am!' he wailed, suddenly. 'Oh, Dustman, don't tell Mrs Tickles, will you? See, here are two pounds for all your trouble. Oh dear, dear, dear, what a stupid fellow I am!'

The dustman took the two pounds, grinned all over his face and went back to his cart, whistling. Mr Tickles went into the house, muttering to himself.

'I'll never forget where I put my green pen again, I never will, never, never, never!'

But I shouldn't be surprised if he forgets again tomorrow, would you?

Good Old Tinker-Dog!

There was once a dog called Tinker. He belonged to Billy Brown, and the two were great friends. Billy had no brothers or sisters to play with, so he played with Tinker-dog instead. He gave him his breakfast and his dinner, and sometimes he even spent his Saturday money on a nice juicy bone for Tinker. So you can see how fond he was of his dog.

Now Tinker was a funny-looking dog. He looked a bit like a collie, a bit like a terrier, and his face was very much like a pug. Billy's mother said he was the ugliest dog she had ever seen, and that made Billy sad.

'Don't take any notice of what people say,' he whispered to Tinker. '*I* think you are the nicest dog in the whole world, Tinker, and you play better than any boy or girl I've ever seen!'

Tinker loved Billy. He loved the little boy so much that he even put up with being bathed, though he did so hate that. It was horrid to stand in hot water and be afraid of soap going in your eyes all the time. But he liked being well brushed every day. He liked to feel his coat silky and smooth, right down to the end of his tail!

One day Billy saw a notice on the wall. It said that there was to be a dog show at a garden fair to be held in the rector's garden. There were to be all sorts of prizes for different kinds of dogs.

'Ooh!' said Billy, in delight. 'Look, Tinker-dog! A dog show! I'll take you, and you're sure to get first prize, a good dog like you!'

So when the day came, Billy asked his mother if she would give him fifty pence, which was what had to be paid to go into the garden fair. 'I'm going to take Tinker-dog to the dog show there,' he said, proudly. 'I'm sure he will win a prize, Mother!'

His mother laughed. 'What, that ugly old Tinker-dog win a prize!' she said. 'No, no, Billy – he never will. He's a nice enough dog for a pet, but he'll never win any prize for you, never!'

Billy said nothing more. He gave Tinker a good brushing, and put on his old collar. He would have liked to buy him a new one but there was no money in his money-box. Then off the two went to the fair in the rectory garden.

Billy paid his fifty pence to the man at the gate, and he and Tinker went inside the lovely garden. There was a big tent in the distance, labelled 'Dog Show', and Billy went over to it.

A lady was at the door, entering the names of all the dog owners who wanted to show their dogs. There were fox terriers, pekes, collies and all kinds of dogs, looking very smart. When Billy's turn came, the lady looked at Tinker.

'But you can't enter *him* for the show,' she said. 'He's a mongrel! He isn't a fox terrier, a peke or a collie, or anything. He's just a funny mixture of all of them! I'm sorry – but I'm afraid it's no use trying to enter such a funny-looking animal.'

'But he's a very, very good dog,' said Billy, almost crying with disappointment. 'Couldn't you give him a chance?'

'I'm afraid not,' said the lady. 'Now move away, please – I must take the name of the boy behind you.'

Billy moved away. He knew he was too big to cry, but he simply couldn't help the tears coming into his eyes. He knew quite well that Tinker was the finest dog in the world, and it was dreadful to hear people saying unkind things about him. He took Tinker to a shady corner, put his arms round the dog's neck and wiped away his tears on his silky coat.

Presently an old man came by and saw the two sitting there. He guessed that Billy had been crying, and he was sorry. He sat down by the little boy and soon Billy had told him about his big disappointment.

'Dear, dear me!' said the old man, shaking his head. 'That's very sad. But, unless I am mistaken, there *is* a competition you can enter your dog for, Billy. I'll just make certain. Stay here for a minute.'

Soon he was back. 'Yes,' he said. 'There is a prize offered for the best-kept dog in the show. Why not put Tinker-dog in for that? He looks very clean indeed to me, and not too fat or too thin – in fact, he's just right!'

Billy cheered up and went with the old man back to the tent. Soon Tinker and a good many other dogs were being walked about in front of two judges – and whatever do you think? Tinker won the first prize for being the best-kept dog!

'He is so clean and so silky,' said one of the judges. 'His teeth are so white, and he is just the right figure, neither too fat nor too thin. He looks such a happy, cheerful dog, too! We are pleased to give him the first prize.'

And what do you think the prize was? Guess! It was ten pounds! Think of that! Billy could hardly believe his eyes when the old man, who happened to be one of the judges, counted ten bright pounds out into his hand.

'Oh, thank you, thank you!' said Billy, his face red with joy. 'I do feel so pleased!'

Tinker-dog wagged his tail hard and licked the old man's hand. He loved anyone who made Billy happy.

'He's a fine dog, a good dog!' said the old man, patting Tinker.

Billy took Tinker home, longing to tell his mother what happened – and on the way he stopped at a shop. He went inside and bought Tinker-dog a fine red collar. You should have seen it!

'Mother, Mother! Tinker's got a prize!' said Billy, rushing indoors. 'Ten whole pounds. See, I've bought him that new red collar. Doesn't he look fine?'

His mother stared at Tinker-dog in surprise. He certainly *did* look fine.

'Well, he's always been a good and loving dog,' she said, 'and he deserves his prize. I'll never say he's ugly again, Billy!'

But Billy doesn't mind a bit now if people call Tinker-dog ugly or funny-looking. He just says: 'Well, he won a prize of ten pounds at a dog show, so he is a very clever dog and I am proud of him.'

And you should see Tinker-dog's tail wagging then! It's a wonder he doesn't wag it off!

Janet and her Friends

Janet always put out the crumbs every morning for the birds – but especially for the little red-breasted robin who stood on the windowsill each day. He looked in at the window with his bright black eyes and trilled a cheery little song as if to say: 'Well, I'm here, I'm here! What about a nice tasty crumb, my dear, my dear!'

One day a dreadful thing happened. The cat jumped up at the robin and caught him! Janet screamed and ran to save him. The cat dropped the bird – but when Janet picked him up, she saw that one of his little legs was hurt.

So, for four days she nursed the robin, and kept him cosily in a small box till he was quite better again. He was very happy, and often trilled to Janet when she came to feed him. He flew off merrily when she let him go, and she was so pleased to see that he could perch just as well as ever, on his two legs.

Now in the early spring-time Janet fell ill. She had to go to bed – and, oh dear me, what a long time she stayed there! Nobody was allowed to see her, and as she couldn't read, the time seemed very dull. She was tired of her dolls, tired of everything. She longed to get up and go and play. She wanted to see people and talk to her friends. But the doctor said no, she must be kept perfectly quiet.

So the little girl grew more and more dull and often cried when she was alone. She sometimes thought of the robin and wondered if he missed her – and one day he came to see her! He *had* missed his little friend, and at last he made up his mind to go and find her. So he hopped on every windowsill and looked in every room – and there, in the small bedroom was Janet, lying flat in bed, crying big tears down her cheeks!

'Trilla, trilla!' sang the robin, outside. He saw that the window was open a little way at the top and he flew up. He sat on the edge of the window and sang again. Janet heard him and was delighted.

'Oh, Robin!' she said. 'I'm so glad to see you. I'm so bored. No one ever comes to see me, and I'm not allowed to get up. Do come and see me every day.'

So after that the robin came to her bedroom every morning. Soon he would fly right inside and sit on the bed, chirping and singing gaily.

Janet loved him very much and looked for him eagerly. She wasn't allowed visitors, she knew, but she meant to have this little robin, all the same! He made her feel so cheerful and happy.

The robin didn't like to see his little friend looking so sad and ill. What could he do to cheer her up? He had just found a dear little wife and he talked to her about it – and she had a wonderful idea!

'My dear,' she said, 'shall we build our nest in Janet's bedroom? You know, if we build it here in the bank, we shall be too busy to go and see her each day and she would miss you dreadfully. But if we could find a good place in her bedroom, we should be in and out all day long, and keep her amused and happy!'

The robin thought that was a splendid idea. So he flew to Janet's bedroom and had a good look round and he thought that the top of the wardrobe would be a splendid place in which to build his nest. It was high up and not likely to be seen.

So, to Janet's great surprise and delight he brought his little wife to her the next day and sang to Janet all about the good idea they had had for their nest. And they began to build it that very same day! Janet soon guessed what they were doing and her cheeks grew red with happiness and her eyes shone. To think that those dear little robins had really chosen her bedroom for a nesting-place! Oh, she did hope that no one would find out. It would be too dreadful if the nest were taken away!

But no one found out for the robins were very careful indeed. They never came into the room when people were there – only when Janet was alone. They built their nest on the wardrobe, so high up that no one but Janet guessed anything about it! They always picked up anything they dropped, leaves or moss, and were careful to leave their new home tidy and neat.

Janet was so happy watching them. She loved to see first one robin and then another flying in at the window with a leaf, or a piece of soft moss for the nest. Then at last the nest was finished. Janet could just see one side of it if she stood up in bed.

'I do wonder if there will be any baby robins!' thought the little girl, excitedly. 'I'm sure the hen robin is laying eggs.'

So she was. She laid four pretty red-brown eggs and then sat on them to keep them warm. Janet watched the little cock robin flying in and out of the window dozens of times a day with a titbit for his small mate. The little girl was very happy and contented now, for there was something to think about and to watch. She had more colour in her cheeks and quite forgot to cry.

Her mother was pleased. 'I can't think what has happened to make Janet so much better,' she said to the doctor. 'She doesn't seem so bored, and she is always smiling. I really think she is much better.'

'She certainly is,' said the doctor. 'There must be some reason why she seems so much brighter lately, but I don't know what it is. Anyway, it is a very good thing!'

And then one day something dreadful happened: Janet's mother thought she would dust the top of the wardrobe, so up she stepped on a chair – and of course she saw the robins' nest on the top of the wardrobe!

'There's a bird sitting on a nest on the top of the wardrobe!' she said. 'What a mess it will make! I shall clear the nest away.'

But then Janet sat up and began to cry bitterly, and said: 'No, no, no! They are *my* robins! I have watched them for a long time, and they have made me so happy. Don't touch the nest, please, please!'

In the middle of all the excitement, in came the doctor. He heard about the nest, and then he turned to Janet. 'So it was the two little robins who made you so happy all this time, was it?' he said. 'They helped you to forget how bored you were, and visited you every day?'

'Yes,' said Janet. 'They made me feel ever so much better. They came and sang to me, and they built their nest there, and I was hoping there were some eggs so that I could see the little ones when they hatched. In the winter I nursed the little cock robin, when he had a bad leg – and now you see, he has been a good friend to me in return!'

'So he has!' said the doctor. 'Well, we'll let the nest stay there, I think. By the time the eggs hatch, Janet, you will be ready to go downstairs again! What do you think of that?'

Janet was delighted. She could keep the robins' nest and see the young ones – and soon she would go downstairs, and then, perhaps, go out. How lovely!

When everyone had gone and she was alone, she called to the robins. 'Robins! Don't be afraid! The doctor knows what good friends you've been to me. Bring up your young ones and then take them into my garden and teach them to sing and fly. I do love you so!'

'Trilla, trilla, and we love you!' said the cock-robin, peeping over the wardrobe. 'There's nothing like helping one another, is there?'

Inside the Doll's House

There was once a small pixie who had a large family of children. They lived in a foxglove, and each child had a flower for itself. But when the flowers fell off the foxglove there was nowhere for the children to sleep!

So the pixie moved to a rose bush. This was prickly, but there were plenty of roses there, opening in the sunshine. Each small pixie took a flower for himself, and for a few days the little family was happy.

Then someone came along with sharp scissors, snipped off the roses and put them into a basket. The pixie children tumbled out quickly, and ran to their mother. She was in despair.

'It's dreadful to have so many children!' she said. 'There doesn't seem anywhere that we can live in comfort. I wish I could get a proper little house, but that's quite impossible.'

'There's a dear little house in that big house over there!' said a passing rabbit. 'I once saw the little girl who lives there carrying this tiny house out into the garden to play with. It's called a doll's house. It would be quite big enough for you and your family, I should think. Why don't you go there?'

The pixie mother was delighted. She went with her children to the big house one night and climbed in at the nursery window. There was a fire in the room and she could quite well see everything. She looked round – and there, in the corner, stood the doll's house! The pixie gave a squeal of delight and ran to it. She opened the front door and went inside.

It was a lovely house. There were six rooms, and a little stair ran up to the bedrooms. The kitchen had a proper stove, and a dresser with plates, cups and saucers. The dining room and drawing room were full of proper furniture, just the right size for the pixies, and the bedrooms had plenty of small white beds.

'Children! Come and see!' cried the mother pixie. The little pixies ran into the house and shouted with joy to see everything.

'Now just get undressed and pop into bed,' said the mother pixie, happily. 'For once we will have a really good night!'

Just as the small pixies were undressing there came a loud knock at the front door. The pixie went to see who was there – and to her surprise, there stood outside a sailor doll, a teddy bear and a golden-haired doll.

'Good evening,' they said, quite politely. 'We have come to see what you are doing in this house. It belongs to Mary Ann, the little girl whose nursery this is. She would be very upset if her nice house was spoilt. We think you had better come out and go away.'

The mother pixie sat down on the front doorstep and cried into her clean white apron. It was too bad to have to turn out just when she had found a house that suited them all so well.

The toys didn't like to see her crying. They felt most uncomfortable. She really seemed a dear little pixie.

'Please don't cry,' said the sailor doll.

'I can't help it,' sobbed the pixie. 'All my tired little pixie children are getting undressed and jumping into those nice little white beds, and I was just making them a chocolate pudding to eat for their suppers. Can't you smell it cooking on the stove?'

The toys could. It *did* smell delicious!

'You shall taste a little,' said the pixie, and she ran to the kitchen. She ladled some of the chocolate pudding into a dish and took it to the toys. They each tasted some and really, it was the nicest pudding they had ever had!

'If you'll let us stay in this house I'll often cook you things,' said the pixie, looking at them with her bright eyes. 'I'll make you cakes when you have birthdays. I'll sew on any buttons, whiskers or eyes that come loose. I'll keep this house spotless and tidy so that Mary Ann will never guess there's a pixie family living here. In the daytime I'll take all my children into the garden, so that no one will see them.'

'Well – ' said the toys, liking the little pixie very much indeed. 'Well – perhaps it would be all right. Stay a week and we'll see!'

So the pixies stayed a week – and you should have seen that doll's house at the end of it. It was spotlessly clean, for all the children scrubbed the floors, swept and dusted very well. All the saucepans and kettles shone like new. The beds were always neatly made after the children had slept in them, and the pixie had even mended a tiny hole in one of the tablecloths – a hole that had been there ever since Christmas!

Each night she cooked something for the toys – and she was a very good cook indeed. Sometimes it was a pudding. Sometimes it was a few buns. Once it was a birthday cake for the brown teddy bear. She knew how to manage the toy stove very well, and it cooked beautifully for her.

'Pixie, we'd like you to stay here,' said the sailor doll, at the end of the week. 'We are very fond of you and your children, and you certainly keep the doll's house even better than Mary Ann does. Stay with us, and let your children come and play in the nursery at night-time, when we toys come alive and have games too.'

So, very gladly, the pixies stayed on in the doll's house – and they are still there! At night the pixie children go for rides in the clockwork train, and ride on the big elephant. They run races with the clockwork mouse and squeal like mice for happiness!

As for the doll's house it is just as spotless as ever, and Mary Ann's mother often says to her: 'Well, really, Mary Ann dear, you *do* keep that house of yours beautifully! I really am proud of you!'

Mary Ann is quite puzzled – for she knows she doesn't do very much to her house. Nobody has told her that a family of pixies live there, for the toys are afraid that if she knew she might be angry. But she wouldn't. She would be just as pleased as you would be, I'm sure!

So if you should happen to know a little girl called Mary Ann, who has a beautiful doll's house, just tell her who lives in it, will you? Won't she get a surprise!

The Cross Little Girl

Belinda was a cross little girl. If things didn't go right she shouted and stamped her foot. If her toys didn't do exactly as she wanted them to she threw them across the room. If she played snakes and ladders and went down the snakes instead of going up the ladders she quite lost her temper and threw the counters into the fire.

So you can guess that her toys, dolls and games didn't like her one bit!

One day Belinda couldn't find a sailor doll she wanted to play with. She hunted all through her toy cupboard, but it wasn't a bit of good, she could *not* find it! Then in a rage she swept every single thing out of the cupboard on to the floor! Crash! Bang! Smash!

The china doll was broken. The little tea-set had its teapot and a cup smashed to bits. The teddy bear hurt its soft nose. The humming-top was dented at one side. Really, it was too bad of Belinda!

Belinda looked at the empty toy cupboard. 'I

think I'll play at houses,' she said. 'I will make the toy cupboard into a little house for myself. That will be fun!'

She opened the door wide and then squeezed herself into the cupboard on the bottom shelf. It just fitted her nicely!

Then a very peculiar thing happened! The teddy bear suddenly jumped up from the floor and shouted loudly. He did make Belinda jump!

'Toys! Quick, let us shut and lock the door on Belinda, and run away from this nursery! We are so badly treated! Let us go to the next-door-neighbour's cottage. He has two kind little children, and they will treat us better than this cross little girl.'

At once all the toys jumped up. The bricks grew legs, the humming-top grew a face, the tea-set grew legs and arms, and all the dolls walked and talked. Belinda could hardly believe her eyes!

She tried to get out of the cupboard, but she was too late. The teddy bear slammed the door, and then click! She heard the key being turned in the lock. She was a prisoner in the toy cupboard!

Belinda banged on the door and shouted, but the toys took no notice. She heard their little pattering feet running to the door and then down the passage outside. Soon there was not a sound to be heard. They had all gone!

Belinda was frightened and angry. It was all very well to play at houses, but it was horrid to be shut up like this so that she couldn't get out. She began to feel very squashed and uncomfortable.

She shook the door and called loudly. 'Help! Mummy! Nanny! Help!'

But nobody came. Mummy was out, and Nanny had gone down the garden to hang up the clothes.

The little girl began to cry. She didn't like being locked in. She didn't like her toys running away. She felt really ashamed. Suppose the next-door-neighbour's children took them in and loved them? They would never want to come back to her.

Belinda shook the cupboard again, but it wasn't a bit of use. The door would *not* open! Then, suddenly, the little girl heard a sound of pattering feet again, and all the toys came back into the nursery! Belinda could hear their little high voices!

She listened – and she found out that the toys had run down the garden path to the next-door-neighbour's cottage – and had met a big dog who chased them away! They had been very much frightened and had run back to the nursery as fast as ever they could!

'Toys! Toys! Let me out, please do!' begged Belinda, shaking the door. 'I know I've been a cross little girl. But I'll be better in future, really I will! Do, do let me out, I'm terribly squashed in here! Don't run away from me again – give me another chance!'

'No!' shouted the toys, all together. 'We shall not give you another chance, Belinda. You have been a cross little girl for so long that we don't think you can ever be anything else! You shall stay there!'

Just at that moment Nanny came running up the stairs, calling, 'Belinda, Belinda!'

'I'm here, Nanny!' cried Belinda. 'Oh, do let me out. I'm in the toy cupboard.'

Nanny unlocked the cupboard and stared at Belinda in surprise.

'How did you get locked in?' she asked.

'The toys locked me in,' said Belinda. 'They said I was a cross little girl. And they tried to run away from me, but Bonzo, the next-door dog, met them and chased them back.'

'The *toys* locked you in,' said Nanny, laughing. 'Whatever will you say next? Don't be so silly, Belinda! You must somehow have slipped the lock yourself from the inside of the cupboard!'

Belinda didn't say any more. But you may be sure of two things – she never got into her toy cupboard again to play houses – and she stopped being a cross little girl, and became good-tempered instead.

And now the toys wouldn't *dream* of running away! They are much too happy!

The Stupid Donkey

There was once a very stupid donkey. His name was Neddy, and he had long grey ears, a pretty grey coat, and a tail that could swish all the flies off his back.

He belonged to Mr Turnabout, and was very fond of his master indeed. But Mr Turnabout was not so fond of Neddy. Neddy really could be so very stupid. Sometimes he would go ambling along the road with Mr Turnabout on his back, and then he would suddenly stop.

'Get on, get on!' Mr Turnabout would say. But no, Neddy wanted to stop, and he might stop there all day long. It was very stupid of him, especially when he chose to stop in the middle of a bridge so that no carts or barrows could get past him.

Then sometimes he wouldn't allow himself to be caught. No – he would gallop round and round the field with Mr Turnabout chasing him for all he was worth, panting and shouting. But he never caught Neddy if the donkey didn't want him to.

There was no doubt about it, Neddy could be a very stupid donkey.

One day Mr Turnabout heard that Old Man Twiddleabout, his cousin, was badly in need of a grey donkey.

'Ha!' said Mr Turnabout at once. 'Ho! I'll take *you* to him, Neddy. You're too stupid for me. Perhaps Old Man Twiddleabout can do something with you – but I doubt it, for a stupider donkey than you I never did see!'

So the next day Mr Turnabout took Neddy and saddled him. Then he jumped up on to his broad back and cantered off. Neddy was sad. He didn't want to leave his good master. He wished that he wasn't so stupid, but it was hard for a little donkey to be clever.

Now the way to Old Man Twiddleabout's lay through the Witch Country. Mr Turnabout wasn't quite sure of his way, and he wasn't quite sure how the witches and wizards would treat him, either. So he went at a smart rate, and hoped that nobody would stop him.

Soon he lost his way. He stopped and looked round. There was no one in sight except an old witch sitting knitting on the edge of the well at the bottom of her garden. She looked at Mr Turnabout with bright green eyes and he didn't like them much. But there was no one else from whom he could ask the way, so he cantered up to her on Neddy.

'Good morning,' he said politely. 'Please could you tell me the way to Old Man Twiddle-about's?'

The witch looked at Mr Turnabout and saw the fat leather bag he carried at his waist. She had heard the chink of money and her eyes gleamed.

'I'll tell you the way but first you must pay me,' she said, knitting hard.

'How much?' asked Mr Turnabout.

'Oh, all the money you have in that bag,' said the witch greedily. Mr Turnabout grew pale.

'I can't give you all that,' he said. The witch dropped her knitting and took up her stick. She was just going to turn poor Mr Turnabout into a jumping frog when the donkey grew tired of waiting. He was thirsty and he wanted to trot down to a pond he could see and have a drink. So he asked for one.

'Hee-haw!' he brayed, suddenly, opening his great mouth. 'Hee-haw!'

The witch gave a jump, and was so startled at the enormous noise that she lost her balance and fell over the edge of the well. Splash! She went into the cold water and began to scream.

'Help! Help! Save me!'

Her servant heard her and came running down the garden path. The donkey hee-hawed again and trotted off to the pond. Mr Turnabout, very thankful that the witch had fallen into the well, and very much afraid that her servant would get her out before he was well away, tugged at the reins and tried to make the donkey gallop off.

But no – Neddy wanted his drink and meant to have it. Only after he had drunk about four gallons did he trot off down the road again – just as the witch's servant pulled her up to the top of the well in the bucket!

'Just like you, Neddy, to want a drink when we might have been turned into frogs and snails any minute,' said Mr Turnabout crossly. 'Get on now, get on!'

Neddy galloped on. Mr Turnabout wondered very much if they were going the right way, but thought they were. Soon he saw a curious figure coming along towards them. It was a dwarf wizard, a small creature with wicked eyes and a crooked nose.

Mr Turnabout wanted to gallop on but the wizard stopped him.

'Not so fast, not so fast,' he said. 'Give me the money out of your wallet.'

'Indeed I won't!' said Mr Turnabout, not

feeling very much afraid of this small wizard. He bent forward and tried to box the wizard's long, sticking-out ears – but at once the little creature changed himself into a tree and Mr Turnabout banged his knuckles hard on the bark, making them bleed. Mr Turnabout was very angry.

The wizard changed himself back to his own shape. 'Give me that money!' he cried, and tried to grab the bag of coins. But Mr Turnabout kicked out with his right foot, meaning to send the dwarf flying head over heels.

But the wizard changed himself into a hard rock and poor Turnabout nearly broke his toes!

'Oh!' he cried, rubbing his foot. 'Ow!'

The dwarf changed back to his own shape and grinned. 'I said, give me your money!' he shouted.

Mr Turnabout leapt off the donkey and rushed at the wizard, trying to clutch him with his hands. But at once the dwarf changed himself into a tall and prickly thistle, and the poor man pricked and scratched his hands terribly.

Neddy the donkey was standing patiently waiting. But when he saw the big thistle he looked at it in surprise and joy. Ha, a thistle was a fine titbit for *him*! Before his master could say a word he began to munch that thistle!

'You're eating the wizard!' said Mr Turnabout, half pleased, half frightened. Then, not knowing what might happen next, he leapt on the donkey's back and tore off down the lane. Neddy was still munching the prickly thistle which certainly tasted rather odd.

On they went again and very soon Mr Turnabout came in sight of his cousin's house, set on a hilltop in the distance. But before he reached it, he came across a greedy old woman, half a witch, powerful and strong.

'Stop!' she cried. 'I want your donkey! Give it to me at once, for I have a long way to go.'

Now Mr Turnabout saw that this old woman was very powerful, and he jumped off the donkey at once and bowed politely.

'Madam,' he said, 'the donkey is for sale. You may have him for seven golden pounds.'

'Fiddlesticks!' said the old woman. 'I'm having him for nothing!' She went to one side of Neddy to climb on his back, but he at once turned round so that he was facing her. He didn't like her. She went round to his side again and once more he turned to face her.

She grew cross and struck him with her big stick. Neddy pricked up his big ears and brayed angrily. As quick as lightning he turned himself about so that his back was towards the witch.

Then he kicked out with his hind feet as hard as he could.

'Whoosh!' The old witch sailed through the air and came down bump about a hundred yards away, so frightened that she at once got up and ran for her life! Neddy gave a contented bray and looked round for his master.

Mr Turnabout was looking at the donkey very strangely. Then he scratched his head, rubbed his nose and pursed up his lips.

'Neddy,' he said, 'are you really stupid, or are you clever? You've got rid of a witch today by tumbling her into a well, you've eaten a wizard, and now you've frightened that powerful old witch.'

'Hee-haw!' said Neddy, pleased, and he whisked his tail so hard that he knocked Mr Turnabout's hat off. But his master didn't seem to mind, he just went on staring at the donkey.

'I can't make you out,' said Mr Turnabout. 'You do seem so stupid at times and yet you do the cleverest things without thinking about them. I think you really *are* clever but are too stupid to know it. Well, well, Neddy, I shan't sell you to my cousin, Mr Twiddleabout. You're too good a friend. Come on, turn round now and we'll gallop home to tea!'

So round they turned, the two of them, and

galloped home at top speed – and not a witch or a wizard dared to stop them!

Which do *you* think Neddy was? Stupid – or clever? I'm sure *I* don't know!

Clever Old Jumbo

There was once a sailor doll who loved frightening people. He used to hide in dark corners, and when the golden-haired doll came by he would jump out at her and shout, 'Boo!' The doll was dreadfully frightened, of course, and ran away as fast as she could.

The sailor doll frightened the teddy bear too, and the pink cat and the blue rabbit. They would be walking along at night, enjoying a talk, when suddenly that sailor would dart out at them, his face shining and his big eyes gleaming. 'Boo!' he would cry, and off they would all run, screaming.

The toys were most annoyed with him. How could they stop him? They made up their minds to beg him to be kinder, but he only laughed at them.

'No!' he said. 'I love playing jokes on you. It's fun to see your scared faces!'

One day, when Jill had taken the sailor doll out for a ride in her pram, the toys had a meeting about him. Jill was the little girl whose nursery they lived in and she would soon be back with the sailor, so they had to hurry up and decide what to do.

'Oh, if only we could think of some way to make him heard wherever he goes!' said the teddy bear. 'Then we should know where he was and not be frightened. But he isn't clockwork so we can't hear his works going round, and he doesn't squeak or do anything like that.'

'It's a pity he doesn't wear a bell, like the blue rabbit does!' said the golden-haired doll. 'We always know when Bunny is coming because his bell rings!'

'Well, can't we make him wear a bell?' said the pink cat.

'Of course not!' said the bear. 'Do you suppose he would let us put a bell on him? Don't be silly!'

'Look here, I've got an idea!' said clever old Jumbo, suddenly. 'Let's have some races or sports, and let him win something. The prize shall be a bell and I'll tie it round his neck and pretend it is a great honour for him. He won't like to refuse – and then we shall always know when he is coming and he won't be able to frighten us any more!'

'But he'll be able to take it off, won't he?' said the doll.

'Ha, I'll tie it too tightly for that!' said Jumbo. 'It will be on a thick string and there will be lots of knots, I can tell you! We'll hide the nursery scissors and he won't be able to cut the string or undo the knots. Ho ho!'

'Sh!' said the pink cat. 'Here comes Jill with the sailor doll.'

The next night the toys held their races. The sailor doll was pleased when he heard about them, for he had long legs and could jump very high indeed. He thought he would be sure to win the high jump.

First there was a long race, three times round the nursery, for clockwork toys. The train, the car and the clockwork mouse went in for that and the train won very easily. The prize was a bit of cottonwool for smoke, and the train tucked it into its funnel and was delighted.

Then there was a running race for ordinary toys. The sailor went in for that but he didn't expect to win it because he knew the pink cat could go very fast. She bounded along and easily won the prize – a piece of blue ribbon.

Then came the jumping. Ah, the sailor was going to win that! He had quite made up his mind. He didn't guess that the other toys had made up their minds he should win it too!

They all jumped – but everyone was careful to jump very low indeed. Only the sailor jumped high – and he certainly jumped twice as high as anyone else! He was very pleased with himself.

'Pooh, what poor jumpers you all are!' he said, proudly looking round. 'No one can beat *me* at jumping. I've won the prize! What is it, please?'

'It's a *beautiful* prize,' said clever Jumbo, coming forward. He held in his trunk a brightly shining little bell. He had taken it off a pair of old reins in the toy cupboard and had polished it up till it shone. The sailor doll looked at it.

'Well – I'm not sure I want that for a prize,' he began.

'Very well,' said Jumbo, at once. 'I'll give it to the blue rabbit. He jumped nearly as high as you did, and I'm sure he tried harder.'

The sailor doll didn't like that. He frowned and sulked. 'That's not true,' he said. 'I jumped twice as high as anyone, and I tried the hardest too. I must have the prize. You are not to give it to the blue rabbit.'

'Very well,' said Jumbo. 'I have much pleasure in giving *you* the prize. Let me tie it round your neck so that everyone can see what an honour you have won!'

The sailor doll came forward, pleased. The old elephant tied the bell tightly round his neck, knotting the stout string a dozen times. The sailor thanked him and walked off. Jingle-jingle-jingle, went the bell! It made a very loud sound indeed!

Well, of course, the sailor doll was never able to frighten anyone after that! Wherever he went the bell shook and jingled, and everyone always knew where he was. It wasn't a bit of good for him to hide any more – his bell rang and warned anyone nearby where he was. Then they called out: 'Oho, we can hear you hiding there! You can't frighten *us*!'

Sailor doll was angry. He tried to undo the knots but he couldn't. He tried to find the nursery scissors but they were well hidden under the doll's house and he didn't know where they were. He asked all the toys, one by one, please to undo the string that tied the bell round his neck – but nobody would.

'I believe you put it there on purpose!' he cried angrily to Jumbo one day.

'Of course I did!' said Jumbo, grinning. 'And it will stay there until you promise never to frighten anyone any more. So now you know!'

Sailor promised yesterday – so the bell is coming off today. But *wasn't* it a good idea of clever old Jumbo's?

A Basket of Brownies

John had a bicycle that his uncle had given him two birthdays ago. When it was new it was very beautiful – as bright as silver, with a fine, tinkling bell, a lamp in front, and a brake under the handle that John used when he was going downhill.

But when two years had gone by it didn't look quite so beautiful. It had been out in the rain and the mud, the bell had got broken, and the lamp wouldn't light. John looked at his bicycle sadly one day and made up his mind to clean it well.

So he asked his mother for some polish, an old cloth and a duster, and set to work. He rubbed the polish on with the cloth, and then made the bicycle shine brightly with the duster. His mother was pleased.

'John, you're a good boy,' she said. 'When you've cleaned up your bicycle nicely I'll give you something new for it!'

John was delighted. He did so badly want a

new bell. Then people would know he was coming when he rang it. So he worked away hard, and by dinner-time the bicycle shone as bright as silver, and looked as good as new. His mother came in from her shopping and looked at it.

'Well done, John,' she said. 'I've brought you back something new to put on your bicycle, as I promised. Here it is!'

She handed John a parcel, quite a big one. He undid it – and what do you think was inside it? Not a bell, but a new basket to go on the front of the bicycle! John was disappointed, but he didn't like to say so.

'Isn't it a nice basket, John?' said his mother. 'I thought it would be so useful when you go shopping for me. You can put all the parcels into the basket and carry them home easily.'

'Thank you very much, Mother,' said John. He fixed the basket on the front of the handle, but he did wish it was a new bell! How nice a fine new, shining bell with a loud ting-a-ling would have been! The basket was all right, but it was a very dull sort of thing.

'Do you want any shopping this afternoon, Mother?' he asked after dinner.

'No, thank you,' said his mother. 'I've done it all this morning. Why don't you go for a ride

to the woods, John? There may be some blackberries there.'

So John set off, his bicycle shining brightly.
He soon came to the woods, for he could pedal
very quickly. He chose a fairly wide path
through the woods so that his bicycle could go
along easily. When he came to a thick clump of
brambles he jumped off. Blackberries! Fine big
ones, black and juicy! John was soon picking
them as fast as he could, and his mouth quickly
became as black as the fruit!

Now as he was busy picking, he suddenly saw
a very strange sight. It was so strange that he
could hardly believe his eyes. He saw, coming
round the blackberry bushes, a line of very
small brownies, each wearing a red tunic and
green stockings. There were about seven of
them, and they seemed in a great hurry. Just as
they came round the bush, they stopped.

'We shall be very late,' said one. 'I am sure we
shall never get there in time.'

'Oh, I don't want to miss the party!' said
another, and took out a small green handkerchief as if he were going to cry.

'It's a pity we got lost this morning,' said the
first one. 'I know the way now, but we are most
certainly very late indeed.'

Suddenly one of the small brownies saw

John's bicycle standing nearby. He pointed to it in excitement.

'Look!' he cried. 'A bicycle! Just what we want! Let's make it small and then perhaps it will carry all of us to the party in good time! I know how to work it.'

The brownies all rushed to the bicycle, and to John's astonishment one of them took up a stick and began to wave it over his bicycle.

'Hi, hi!' shouted John, suddenly, coming out from behind the bush. 'Don't do that! That's *my* bicycle! If you make it small I shan't be able to ride it. You mustn't do that. It isn't yours!'

The brownies looked round in a fright. When they saw that John looked a kindly little boy they didn't run away, but just looked sorrowfully at the bicycle. What a pity they couldn't use it after all!

'How disappointing!' said one with a sigh 'I did think we had found a way to get to the party in time. Won't you really let us make the bicycle small, little boy? We'd make it big again later on.'

'I'd really rather you didn't,' said John. 'You see, I've only just cleaned it today, and I'm rather proud of it. I should be very upset if you made it small and forgot to make it big again. It wouldn't be any use to me at all.'

'Well, we *might* forget, in the excitement of the party,' said one of the brownies. 'We haven't very good memories. We'd better go on our way, I think.'

The little folk were just turning to go when a great idea came to John. 'Wait! Wait!' he cried. '*I* could take you to your party! I could put you all comfortably into my new basket in front there; it's quite big enough, for you are so tiny! Then, if you could tell me the way, we'd soon be there!'

The brownies began to twitter like birds in their excitement. 'Yes, yes!' they cried. 'Take us, little boy! We can easily squeeze ourselves into your basket!'

So John picked up each brownie very carefully, in his hands and put them all into his fine new basket. How pleased he was to have a basket then! When each tiny fellow was in the basket, he got on the saddle and put his feet on the pedals.

'Now you must tell me the way,' he said.

One of the brownies stood up in the basket and pointed the way to go. Off went John. The path grew rather narrow but on he went. The brownies knew the way quite well, and John pedalled fast. Down this path – and down that – round this tree – and round that one. And

suddenly they were there! There was no doubt
about it, for, in a grassy clearing, there ran and
chattered scores of fairy folk – brownies, pixies,
gnomes and many others. How John stared!

'Thank you very much, little boy,' said the
brownies, scrambling out of the basket, and
sliding down the front part of the bicycle. 'You
shall have your reward! Now do you mind going
home, because the other little folk might be
frightened to see you here!'

'Well – I'm afraid I don't know the way,' said
John. 'You see, there were so many twists and
turns!'

'Oh, your bicycle knows the way,' said a
brownie, and he gave the wheels a push. 'Home,
bicycle, home!'

To John's surprise the bicycle turned itself
round, and, with him on the saddle, pedalled
itself merrily, shot up this path and that, and in
a very short while came out into the place where
John had been picking blackberries. There it
stopped.

'Well, that was a most extraordinary adventure really!' thought John, as he got off to pick
some more blackberries. 'I've never seen fairies
before, and never thought I should, though I've
looked for them often enough! I'm afraid no one
will believe me if I tell them! I don't think I'll

say anything to anyone about it.'

But he had to – because the very next morning, when he went to get out his bicycle, what do you think was fixed to the handle? Why, the finest, biggest silver bell John had ever seen, and when he rang it, goodness, what a noise! You could hear it a mile away!

There was a small label on it and John read it. It said: 'From seven grateful brownies' – so there was no need to wonder where it came from!

Of course everyone wanted to know where John had got his beautiful bell, and he had to tell them. He told *me*, so that's how I know. I *wish* I'd seen that basketful of brownies, don't you?

The Very Fine Tail

There was once a small lizard who had a remarkably fine tail. It was long and graceful, and Flick the lizard was very proud of it. The other lizards had tails too, but none were quite so fine as his.

The lizards used to play together on a sunny bank, and Flick always showed off his tail as much as he could. The others became tired of hearing about the wonderful tail and laughed at Flick.

'Pride goes before a fall!' they said. 'You be careful that nothing happens to that tail of yours! If it's so grand it may be stolen!'

'Don't be foolish!' said Flick, quite offended. 'Who would steal a lizard's tail?'

'Ah! You never know!' said the others.

When the autumn came, and the nights were chilly, the little lizards began to think of finding a nice cosy hole in which they could sleep the winter away. They peered under stones, they looked into all the holes on the bankside to see which would be best. Flick was too lazy to help.

He lay on the bank in the autumn sunshine, spreading out his long, graceful tail for all the birds and the mice to see.

He fell asleep as he lay there. He didn't hear the excited squeals of the other lizards. He didn't hear the squeaks of the mice as they scurried over the bank, frightened. He didn't even hear the deep, warning croak of the big old toad who sat all day under his damp stone, peering out at the sunny world outside.

'Rat!' squealed the lizards, and rushed for their hole.

'Rat, rat!' squealed the mice, and scurried away.

'Here comes the wicked rat!' croaked the old toad, who knew that the lean brown rat would gobble up any small creature he came across. 'Beware of the rat!'

The rat appeared on the bank, his whiskers twitching. He could smell lizard. Ah, he would dearly love a dinner of nice fat lizard. Then, to his great delight he spied the sleeping lizard just nearby, lying in the short grass, his long tail proudly spread out beside him.

He was just about to pounce on the sleeping creature when all the other lizards, peeping from their hole, squealed to Flick in fright.

'Flick! Flick! Run quickly! The RAT is here!'

Flick woke with a jump. Did he hear someone say RAT? He swung round – and saw the lean grey-brown rat just about to pounce on him.

He tried to run – but he was too late. The rat jumped and caught Flick by his beautiful tail. Flick wriggled in pain but he could not get away.

'Leave your tail behind and run to your hole,' said the old, wise toad. 'Go on! Break it off and leave it. Then you will escape!'

Poor Flick! There was nothing else to be done! He snapped off his tail, and then rushed to his hole, a funny little short-bodied lizard with no tail at all!

The rat was astonished. He was about to rush after Flick when he felt the tail jumping about between his paws. He gobbled it up and then went on his way, sorry that he hadn't eaten the rest of the little lizard.

Then how sad and upset Flick was! He had no beautiful tail. He didn't look like a lizard. He moped in his hole and the others were sorry for him.

'We always told you something would happen to that tail you were so proud of,' they said. 'But cheer up, Flick – it's no use moping. You were foolish about your tail when you had it – don't be foolish about it now it's gone!'

So Flick cheered up and went to help the others to find a nice winter hole. When the little lizards found one they all crowded into it, and, curling themselves up together, fell fast asleep. They did not wake until the warm days came again – and then what a surprise Flick got!

His tail had grown again while he had slept! Would you believe it! It was not so fine nor so long as his first tail. It was short and stumpy, and it didn't seem to fit him very well – but at any rate it was a *tail*! Flick was very happy. He ran about with the others squealing. He helped them when he could, and was more friendly than he had ever been before.

'It's a good thing you lost that old tail of yours, Flick!' said the wise old toad. 'You don't *look* so fine with your new one – but you're a much *nicer* little lizard!'

Mr Stupid and Too-Smart

One day Too-Smart and his friend Tiny the gnome were walking down the road together. Over Tiny's shoulder was an empty sack which should have been full of potatoes – but Too-Smart and Tiny had earned no money that day, so they had not been able to buy the potatoes they wanted.

Now just as they came up to a field-gate who should they see coming out of the field but Mr Stupid, the brownie farmer, carrying over his shoulder a big sack full of something heavy. Too-Smart took a look into the field. It was a potato field. Mr Stupid must have been digging up a sack of potatoes to take home.

'Look!' said Too-Smart, nudging Tiny. 'See that sack of potatoes on old Stupid's back? I've got a plan to get them all from him! Ho ho! All you've got to do is walk behind a little way and pick up what falls out of the sack. See? *I'll* manage the rest!'

Up he went to Mr Stupid and bade him

good-day. Stupid was going very slowly indeed for the sack was too heavy, and bent him double.

'That's a heavy load you've got!' said Too-Smart, brightly. 'If you promise to give me a basket of carrots, Mr Stupid, I'll wish a wish for you so that your load becomes lighter every step you take!'

Mr Stupid mopped his forehead with his big red handkerchief. The sack was terribly heavy. He looked sideways at Too-Smart and grinned. 'All right,' he said. 'You lighten my load for me and maybe I'll give you a basket of carrots.'

'I'll just tap your sack then as I wish,' said Too-Smart. He waited until Mr Stupid came to a grassy path that led up the hillside to his house, for he did not want the old farmer to hear the potatoes dropping out on the road. Then he pretended to tap the sack smartly, but what he really did was to cut a hole at the bottom of it with his knife.

'I wish your load may become lighter and lighter!' he said. 'There you are, Mr Stupid. Now you'll soon find that my wish will work for you.'

The two went on up the hill together, and Too-Smart talked hard all the time to hide the soft plop-plop as something fell out of the sack at every step. Behind them stepped Tiny, with *his* sack – but to his great astonishment he found that it was not potatoes that fell from Mr Stupid's sack – it was stones! He couldn't think what to do – he couldn't possibly tell Too-Smart, for then Stupid would hear.

'Well, I'd better pick up the stones and put them in my sack, I suppose,' thought Tiny. 'Then I can show them to Too-Smart if he doesn't believe me when I say that no potatoes fell from Stupid's sack.'

So the small gnome picked up every stone that fell from Mr Stupid's sack, and put them into his own. Goodness, how heavy they were!

'Well, Mr Stupid, is your load feeling any lighter?' asked Too-Smart, as he walked up the hill beside Mr Stupid.

'Oh, *much* lighter!' said Mr Stupid. 'Dear me, it's wonderful, Too-Smart. I am very glad I met you, really.'

'So am I,' said Too-Smart. 'I do like doing anyone a good turn. I told you your load would get lighter, and I've kept my word. I'm a smart chap, Mr Stupid.'

'There's no doubt about it,' said the old farmer, grinning to himself as he heard the soft plop of one stone after another tumbling out of his sack. He knew quite well that there must be

someone behind picking them all up. Well, well, if Too-Smart thought his sack had potatoes in it, that was his own look-out! Ho ho!

Poor little Tiny panted behind them, picking up more and more stones. His sack became very heavy indeed and he could hardly carry it, for he was not very big. As for Mr Stupid's sack, it was soon as light as a feather!

When at last he and Too-Smart arrived at his house, Mr Stupid put down his sack without looking at it. He turned to Too-Smart with a smile.

'Well, you certainly kept your word,' he said. 'My load is much lighter now. I hardly felt it, coming up the hill. Wait here a moment and I'll get you your reward – a basket of carrots.'

He went indoors, and no sooner had he gone than Too-Smart ran eagerly to Tiny, who was standing gloomily by the gate with his enormous sack of stones.

'What did I tell you?' he whispered. 'Am I not a smart chap, Tiny?'

'Not so very,' said the little gnome sulkily. 'I suppose you know that that was a sack of *stones*, not potatoes, that old Stupid was carrying? If you don't believe me, look inside my sack. I've picked them all up and carried them. My goodness, my back is nearly broken!'

Too-Smart stared at the stones in horror. Stones! Not potatoes! Whoever would have thought of that?

Just then Mr Stupid came out with a basket of very old, very hard carrots. He walked up to Too-Smart and Tiny.

'Well?' he said to Tiny. 'Did you pick up all my stones and carry them home for me? It really was very kind of you, and *such* a good idea of Too-Smart's! I can't imagine how you thought of it, but I am most grateful. My wife asked me to bring home a sack of flints to edge her new flower garden, and I can tell you it was a terrible load to carry. I was *so* pleased when kind Too-Smart offered to lighten the load for me! Thank you very much indeed!'

'B-b-b-b-b-ut . . .' began Tiny, in anger and surprise, furious to think he had carried the stones all the way home instead of the farmer. 'B-b-but I thought . . .'

'I don't care what you thought,' said Mr Stupid, kindly. 'It was really very nice of you both. Here is your reward, Too-Smart – a basket of carrots.'

He held out the basket, and Too-Smart saw what nasty old ones they were.

'You ought to be ashamed to give us those horrid carrots!' said Too-Smart angrily.

'Oh, donkeys don't mind if carrots are old or new,' said Mr Stupid, cheerfully. 'I don't expect either of *you* will notice the difference, Too-Smart!'

Mr Stupid picked up Tiny's sack of stones, emptied them out by the side of his wife's flower garden, and gave him back the sack with a grin.

'Goodbye,' he said to the angry gnomes. 'Stupid may be my name – but it isn't my nature, you know! *Good*bye!'

He went indoors, chuckling, and soon Too-Smart and Tiny heard him and his wife roaring with laughter – and they knew why. They went home down the hill in silence, and for a long time after that Too-Smart didn't try any tricks at all.

But I've no doubt he will soon again – don't you think so?

The Little Boy Who Cried

Doreen and Harry were very happy. They had two pounds between them, and they were going to buy a new paint-box. They both loved painting, but their paint-box was very old and not very good – and at last they had saved up two pounds to buy one they had seen in the toy-shop. It was not a very big one, but the colours in it were good and there were two paint-brushes as well.

Harry had the money in his pocket, and he carried a parcel in his hand. Mummy had asked him to take her shoes to be mended. The cobbler lived next door to the toy-shop, so Harry said of course he would take the shoes.

They went on down the road, and passed the park on their way. Running in through the gates was a little boy. Just as the children passed the gates the small boy tripped over something and fell flat on his face. A parcel he carried burst open and out fell sandwiches, an orange, and a sticky piece of chocolate cake.

The children heard a tinkle too, as if a coin has fallen and rollen away – and at the same moment the small boy began to howl. Goodness, how he yelled! You would have thought there were six little boys crying instead of only one!

Doreen couldn't bear to hear anyone cry. She ran up to the little boy and picked him up. He had hurt his knee, and grazed his hands.

'Don't cry,' said Doreen, dusting his jacket down. 'You're not much hurt.'

'B-b-b-b-but my d-d-dinner's all spoilt,' wept the little boy, 'and my m-m-m-money's gone!'

Harry picked up the sandwiches, the orange and the chocolate cake – but they were no good for eating. The orange had burst, the sandwiches had fallen into a puddle and the piece of cake was covered with mud. The little boy's dinner certainly *was* spoilt!

'I had fifty pence in my hand and that fell and rolled down the drain there!' wept the little boy. 'Oh dear! How am I to get home? It's the first time my mother has let me go out alone, and she gave me my dinner to bring to the park and let me have fifty pence to pay for some lemonade and my bus-fare home.'

Doreen and Harry didn't know what to do. The small boy would *not* stop crying. It really was dreadful to hear him.

'Listen!' said Doreen, suddenly. 'If you'll stop crying, little boy, we'll buy you some new dinner, and give you the money to get home. We've two pounds between us. We were going to buy a new paint-box, but we'll give you some of the money if you'll cheer up.'

The little boy wiped his eyes and looked at Doreen with a smile. He slipped his hand into hers and squeezed hard.

'I like you,' he said. 'You are kind. Tell me your name and I'll ask my Mummy to send you back the money.'

'Oh no,' said Doreen. 'You needn't bother about that. We can spare you the money because it is our very own.'

Harry took the small boy to the water fountain and bathed his knee and hands. Then they went with him to a baker's shop, and bought him two buns, a cherry-cake and a bottle of lemonade. Then they bought an apple at another shop. Harry unwrapped his mother's shoes and carefully wrapped up all the food they had bought, in the brown paper. He was very much afraid the little boy would fall down again and spoil everything!

'There you are!' he said. 'There's a fine lunch for you! I should go and sit down on that seat by the duck-pond, if I were you, when you eat it.

Then you can watch the ducks.'

'How much is your bus-fare home?' asked Doreen.

'Twenty pence,' said the small boy.

'Well, here you are,' said Harry, giving the little fellow the money. 'Put that in your pocket and keep it safely till your bus comes. I'm sorry we can't stop any longer with you, but our mother will worry if we are too long. Goodbye!'

Doreen and Harry left the little boy sitting happily on a seat with his lunch in the brown paper. They took their mother's shoes to be mended, and then they looked into the shop next door. There was that lovely paint-box!

'We can't have it after all,' said Doreen. 'It's a pity, Harry – but we had to help the little boy who cried, didn't we?'

'Of course,' said Harry. He felt in his pocket and found three twenty pence pieces, which was all that was left of the money he had had. 'Look, Doreen – we've still got sixty pence left. Shall we put it back in our money-box or shall we spend it on something now?'

'Oh, let's spend it now,' said Doreen. 'It will take too long to save up two pounds again! Let's buy an ice-cream each and take some sweets home to Mummy!'

So they had an ice-cream each and bought some peppermints to take home to their mother because she was so fond of them. They told her all about the little boy who cried, and she was pleased when she heard how kind they had been.

'But we couldn't get that paint-box we wanted!' said Harry, with a sigh.

'Never mind,' said their mother. 'Your kindness is worth far more than a paint-box!'

Two days later, when Doreen and Harry were playing in the garden, a little car pulled up outside their door, and out jumped a pretty lady. She had a big parcel in her hand and she ran up to the front door with it. She knocked and the children's mother opened the door.

'Oh, good morning!' said the lady. 'Does Mrs White live here?'

'Yes – I'm Mrs White,' said the children's mother.

'Well, your two children were *very* kind to my little boy the other day in the park,' said the lady. 'He fell down and spoilt his lunch and lost his money – and they bought him another lunch and gave him the money to catch his bus home. He told me all about it – and he told me too that they really meant to buy a paint-box with the money they so kindly gave him, so, in return for their kindness, I've brought them a little present!'

'Oh, how nice of you!' cried Mrs White. 'Doreen! Harry! Come here a minute!'

The children came running. Their mother told them who the lady was, and what she had come to bring. The lady smiled at them and gave them the parcel – and whatever do you think was inside when they opened it?

There were two big, beautiful paint-boxes, one for each of them, and two fine painting-books! The paint-boxes were *very* much nicer than the one that the children had been going to buy and they were full of excitement when they saw them.

'Oh, thank you, thank you!' cried Harry. 'But how *did* you know our name and where we lived? We didn't tell your little boy.'

'No – but you wrapped up his lunch in a nice piece of brown paper for him – and on the paper was your mother's name and address!' said the lady. 'So that's how I knew, you see – and I *was* glad because I did so badly want to give you some reward for your kindness! Will you come to tea with Eric tomorrow? He very much wants to see you again. I will come and fetch you in my car if your mother will let you come.'

So tomorrow Doreen and Harry are going to

tea with Eric – but today they are going to do some painting with their beautiful new paint-boxes. They *are* pleased.

'Aren't we lucky!' cried Doreen.

'Yes – but you deserve your good luck!' said her mother. And so they did!

The Pink Teddy Bear

Once there was a pink teddy bear called
Edward. He was quite big, his whiskers were
very fine and he had two odd eyes, for one was a
brown boot-button and the other was a black
one. But he could see very well indeed.

He belonged to Elsie, and she often played
with him. Each morning he went for a ride in
her doll's pram, and each evening he was put to
bed in a doll's cot, so you can see he was a very
lucky bear.

One afternoon Elsie took him out into the
garden, and had a tea-party. There was herself,
the little boy next door, the black kitten and
Edward the teddy bear. They each had a cup
and saucer and a plate, and real biscuits to eat
and real milk to pour out of the teapot. So it was
a most exciting party.

'You must clear away everything tidily!'
called Elsie's mother, when they had finished.
'It is nearly bedtime, but you've just time to tidy
up the garden, and to wash up the tea things.'

Elsie carried the tea things indoors and the black kitten came with her. The little boy next door helped Elsie to wash the plates and cups, and then it was time for him to go home. He called goodbye and ran off.

'Good girl, Elsie,' said her mother, when she saw how nicely Elsie had washed up. She hadn't broken anything at all. 'Now run into the bathroom and turn on the hot tap for your bath.'

Elsie loved doing that, so off she went – and do you know she quite forgot that there was one thing she hadn't brought in from the garden – and that was poor Edward, the bear!

There he sat at the bottom of the garden on the damp grass, all alone. He was very cross with Elsie for forgetting him. Tears came into his boot-button eyes when he saw the light go on in the bathroom and heard the splash of the bath-water.

'Elsie's going to have her bath,' he thought. 'She's forgotten all about me! How horrid of her!'

Elsie had her bath, and then said her prayers and jumped into bed. She was very sleepy. It wasn't long before her eyes closed and she fell fast asleep.

But Edward didn't fall asleep. No, he was far too frightened! A great big thing had just flown over him and shouted, 'Too-whit, too-whoo!' right in his ear! Then a big prickly creature ran into him and scratched him. Edward cried out in pain, but the hedgehog didn't even say it was sorry.

'You shouldn't sit there, right in my way,' it said, rudely, and went on down the garden.

After that a spider ran over Edward's head and began to spin a web between his ears. Edward was very angry. His arms were much too short to brush away the web, and the spider wouldn't stop when he told it he was a teddy bear.

'I don't care what you are!' said the spider. 'I'm going to make my web here!'

Now, in the middle of the night, Elsie suddenly woke up – and she remembered Edward, her bear. She hadn't put him to bed in his nice warm cot! Goodness gracious, where was he? 'Oh, I must have left him out in the garden!' she thought, and she sat up in bed in horror. 'Poor Edward! He will be so sad and lonely! I must go and fetch him.'

So Elsie put on her dressing-gown, and her little red slippers, and down the stairs she crept. She opened the garden door and went into the garden.

It looked so different at night! It was so very

dark, and the grass was so wet. She tried to find the path and at last found herself walking on it. Twigs brushed against her face and frightened her. Soon she had lost the path and was on the wet grass again. She didn't know where she was at all!

'Well, I'm in the garden, I know!' said Elsie. 'But what part of it? Oh, I do hope I don't fall into the pond! It's so dark I can't see where I'm going!'

She tripped over a stone and hurt her foot. Then she walked straight into a tree and bumped her head. She was just rubbing it when a big bird flew near her, crying: 'Too-whit, too-whoo!' at the top of its voice.

'Oh, owl, don't frighten me so!' said poor Elsie. She sank down on the wet grass and began to cry. It was dreadful – she didn't dare to go any further, for fear of falling over or of bumping her head!

Now Edward the bear was not far off. He was frightened out of his life because a big beetle, two earwigs, a mouse and a rat had all run over him, and he hardly dared to move. But when he heard the sound of Elsie crying he forgot all about his fears.

'Why, that's Elsie!' he thought. 'She's crying! She must have remembered me and come out to look for me in the dark – and she's lost herself! Poor little girl, how frightened and lonely she will be, with all these night-time creatures about. I wouldn't like a spider to make a web between *her* ears, or a rat to nibble at her nose. I must go and find her.'

Up got the brave little bear, and, listening to the sound of Elsie's sobs, he began to make his way to where she was sitting. How he bumped his nose when he walked into trees! How wet his feet were! How he scratched himself when he fell into a rose bush! But never mind, he was getting nearer to Elsie.

Suddenly the frightened little girl felt a small furry paw pushed into her hand, and the growly voice of the teddy bear spoke to her.

'Don't cry, Elsie. I heard you, and I've come to find you.'

'Oh, Edward! Is it really you?' said Elsie, astonished and glad. 'I came out to find *you* and you've found me instead! Oh, you *are* a dear! Do you know the way indoors?'

'We'll find it together,' said Edward. So hand in hand the two stumbled up the garden, not at all frightened now they had one another. They soon found the garden door and crept indoors. They went upstairs and Elsie hopped into bed.

'You shall sleep with *me* tonight, Edward,'

she said. 'Your poor feet are so cold and wet. I'll warm them for you.'

So the two fell asleep together, and Edward's feet soon got dry and warm. He was so happy and excited.

'What an adventure to tell the toys to-morrow!' he thought. 'None of them has ever slept in Elsie's bed before. How glad I am she forgot me and left me out in the garden! Now I know how much she loves me!'

In the morning when Elsie woke up, the bear was still in her bed. She looked at him and remembered what had happened in the night.

'Did it really happen, or did I dream it?' she wondered. 'Oh, Edward, you were alive last night and came to find me in the garden. You are a most *wonderful* teddy bear!'

And now Edward almost hopes he will be left out again – but I don't expect Elsie will ever forget him another time, do you?

When the Stars Fell Down

On Guy Fawkes night little Tweeky the pixie was sitting by a puddle in the lane, eating a late supper of honey and cobweb-bread. He didn't know it was Guy Fawkes night. He didn't know anything about fireworks at all.

So when he heard a rocket go up he nearly jumped out of his skin, and he dropped a large piece of cobweb-bread into the puddle. He was most upset.

He looked up into the sky. To his enormous suprise he saw a crowd of coloured stars dropping out of the black sky towards him. They were the stars out of the rocket, but he didn't know it. He thought they were real stars falling out of the sky, and he was frightened.

He dived under a bush and stayed there for two minutes, shivering. Then he crawled out. Where had those stars fallen? They must be somewhere about.

He began to look. He hunted over the grass at the lane-side. He searched among the stones in

the road. He climbed up the bare hedge and looked along the top. No stars anywhere. Wherever could they be?

Then he thought of looking in the puddle. So he ran to it and looked into the water. Reflected there were the real stars that were shining high up in the sky. But Tweeky at once thought that they were the coloured stars he had seen falling down.

'They've dropped into this puddle!' he shouted in excitement. 'They've fallen splash into this water! Now I will get them out, thread them on a string and give them to the fairy queen for a birthday present. Oh, what a marvellous thing! They have all dropped into the puddle!'

He ran off and presently came back with a net. He put it into the puddle and tried to catch the stars. He seemed to get them easily in his net, but as soon as he took the net out, alas! there were no stars there at all. It was most annoying.

Soon Grass-Green the goblin came by, and looked astonished to see Tweeky fishing in the pool.

'What do you fish for?' he asked.

'Stars!' said Tweeky, proudly. 'They fell from the sky into this puddle as I was eating my supper. Red, green and blue they were – the most beautiful stars I have ever seen.'

'What a surprising thing!' said Grass-Green, peering into the puddle. It was all stirred up with Tweeky's fishing, and he couldn't see anything at all. But he wanted those stars very badly indeed. So he knelt down by the puddle and began to feel in the water with his hands.

'You're not to take my stars!' shouted Tweeky in a rage. 'You're a robber, Grass-Green! Leave my stars alone!'

Pinkity the elf heard Tweeky shouting and came to see what the matter was.

'Tell Grass-Green to go away!' cried Tweeky. 'He is trying to steal my stars. A whole lot fell into this puddle while I was eating my supper. They are mine! I want to thread them on a string and give them to the queen for her birthday.'

'Nonsense!' said Pinkity, at once. 'The puddle isn't yours, Tweeky. If Grass-Green wants to fish in it, of course he can do so! *I* shall fish too, and if I find the stars, they shall be mine! Make room, Grass-Green!'

Grass-Green wouldn't make room, and soon there was such a shouting and a squabbling that it woke up Old Man Pinny-Penny, who was asleep under the hedge not far off. He was half a gnome and half a goblin, and he had a fearful temper. He sat up and scowled.

'Who's making all that noise?' he grunted. 'I'll teach them to scream and squabble at night! I'll knock their heads together! I'll spank them! I'll – I'll – I'll . . .'

Dear me, the things Old Man Pinny-Penny was going to do would fill a book and a half! He got up, and went to the puddle round which Tweeky, Grass-Green and Pinkity were all pushing and squabbling.

'WHAT'S all this?' shouted Pinny-Penny, in his very biggest voice. 'How DARE you wake me up?'

'Ooh!' cried Tweeky in fright. 'We didn't mean to disturb you, Pinny-Penny. We will be quiet. But oh, it is so annoying of Grass-Green and Pinkity, because they are trying to steal my stars.'

'Steal your stars?' cried Old Man Pinny-Penny. 'Now what in the wide world do you mean, Tweeky?'

'Well, a whole lot of beautiful coloured stars fell out of the sky while I was eating my supper by the puddle,' said Tweeky, 'and when I looked I saw they had fallen into the puddle. So I went to get a net to fish them out. Then I shall thread them and make them into a necklace for the queen.'

Grass-Green scooped through the puddle with his big hands, and Tweeky smacked him on the head. He hit back at the pixie, and struck Pinkity instead, splashing him from head to foot. Pinkity danced with rage and hit out with both his fists – but oh, my goodness me, he hit Old Man Pinny-Penny by mistake, and didn't that make him angry!

With a shout of rage he picked up Pinkity and sat him down in the very middle of the pool! He pushed Grass-Green who fell on his face in the puddle, and as for Tweeky, he found himself rolling over and over in the water, his mouth full of mud!

How they howled! How they roared! They picked themselves up out of the puddle and shook the water from them like dogs. Then, still howling, and shivering from head to foot, they ran off to get dry, leaving Old Man Pinny-Penny alone by the big puddle. He looked into it as soon as it had become smooth and quiet, and sure enough, he saw the stars reflected there.

'Goodness!' said Old Man Pinny-Penny, in astonishment. 'So Tweeky spoke the truth. There *are* stars there after all! I'll go and get my net.'

Off he went – but before he came back a grey donkey wandered down that way and saw the puddle shining. He was thirsty so he went to it and drank. He drank and drank and drank – and by the time he had finished there was no puddle at all! It had all gone down his throat, stars and all!

When Old Man Pinny-Penny came back he couldn't find the puddle, though he looked up and down the lane from end to end.

'The stars have flown back to the sky and taken the puddle with them,' he thought mournfully. 'What a pity!'

The grey donkey watched him looking for the puddle, and he thought it was very funny to see Pinny-Penny looking for a puddle that was down his throat. So he threw back his head and laughed loudly.

'Hee-haw! Hee-hee-haw!'

But Old Man Pinny-Penny didn't know what the joke was!

Poor Mr Greedy!

There was once a sharp little pixie called Nab. He lived just on the edge of Giantland, and if there was one thing he liked more than another it was going to the nearest giant's pea-patch and taking a few peas when they were ripe. They were as big as cricket-balls to the pixie, and two of them made a fine dinner for him, cooked with a sprig of mint, and well-buttered when hot.

The pea-patch belonged to Big-Eyes the giant. He could well have spared Nab a few peas now and again, but he was a mean giant, and if he could have counted his peas every day to see that none were missing, he would have done so! As it was he kept a sharp look-out for little Nab, and meant to catch him if he possibly could.

Nab used to slip through the hedge early in the morning before the giant was up. He would slit a big pod with his knife and take out two or three peas. Then back through the hedge he would go, chuckling to think of the giant fast asleep in bed. It was naughty of Nab, and all his friends used to tell him that one day he would surely be caught.

Well, that day came! As he slipped through the hedge early one morning, a big hand came down on him – and goodness me, it was Big-Eyes the giant! He had come out early that day, and had spied Nab running through the fields a long way off. Now he had him at last.

'Oho!' said the giant, in his big voice. 'So I've caught you, Nab! Well, you've often cooked my peas for your dinner – and now perhaps I'll cook *you* for mine.'

Dear me, that did make Nab shiver and shake! The giant had a sack beside him, that he was going to use for his potatoes. He threw Nab into it, tied the neck up tightly, and flung the sack back on the ground.

'You can stay there for a while,' he said. 'I'm going back to my breakfast, and I don't want to let my wife know I've caught you, for she's tender-hearted and might set you free!'

Off he went down the garden, leaving poor Nab wriggling in the sack. Big-Eyes had taken his knife from him, so he could not make a hole with it. He wriggled about until he found a little hole, and then he put his eye to that and peeped through it. At first he could see nothing but the pea-patch.

Then he saw something else. It was a gnome marching along the path, whistling gaily. The gnome was big and fat, and he had mean little eyes set close together. Nab knew him quite well. He was shoemaker to Big-Eyes the giant, who was very fond of him and vowed that Mr Greedy the gnome could make better shoes than anyone else in the kingdom. The two were great friends, though all the rest of the pixies and gnomes hated Mr Greedy, for he was so mean and so very selfish and greedy.

Mr Greedy saw the sack and stirred it with his foot, wondering if there was anything to eat in it. Nab gave a squeal, and Mr Greedy looked astonished.

'Who's there?' he asked.

'Nab, the pixie,' answered Nab.

'What are you doing in that dirty old sack?' asked Greedy, in surprise.

Nab wasn't going to tell him. 'Never you mind!' he said. That made Greedy most curious.

'I believe Big-Eyes the giant has set you to watch his pea-patch for him,' he said. 'Yes, that's what you're doing – and I guess he is paying you a lot of money for it, isn't he?'

'Never you mind, Mr Greedy!' said Nab again.

'Well, I should like to know why Big-Eyes

didn't give *me* the job!' said Greedy, half-sulkily. 'We're great friends, he and I. I would have liked to earn a bit of money watching his peas for him.'

'Well, would you like to change places with me?' suddenly said Nab, watching Mister Greedy through the little hole. 'I'm tired of being in this dark sack. You can have the job of watching Big-Eyes' peas if you want to. I'm sure I don't want to have anything more to do with them!'

'Oh, you always were a lazy little creature!' said Greedy. 'Of course I'll change places with you. I'd enjoy the job very much, and I shan't give you any of the money I get, so there!'

'I don't want any!' said Nab. 'Come on, undo the sack, Greedy.'

Greedy undid the sack, grumbling at the knots. At last the sack was open and Nab joyfully crawled out. He took a quick look round and then fled for the hole in the hedge. He hid there until Greedy had crawled into the sack, and then he ran to him and quickly knotted the string round the neck. Then, chuckling hard, he rushed through the hedge and ran home, vowing to himself that never, never, never would he steal peas again.

Greedy found the sack very dark and stuffy.

No one came to steal the peas. It was very dull. He thought it was a horrid sort of job and he didn't wonder that Nab had given it up so easily.

'I wonder how much Big-Eyes was going to give him,' he thought. 'I'll make him give me double!'

After a while, along came the giant. He picked up the sack and swung it over his shoulder. He carried it up the path, not listening at all to the cries of pain that Mister Greedy kept making as he was bumped here and there.

Big-Eyes reached the kitchen and flung the sack down on the floor.

'Hey, cook!' he called to his servant. 'Here's something for you to cook for my dinner!'

Greedy cried out in fright. The giant went out of the kitchen and the cook undid the sack. She hauled the frightened gnome out by the scruff of the neck and put him on the table.

Greedy at once leapt off and ran to the dining-room, where the giant was just taking off his big boots.

'Big-Eyes!' shouted Greedy, in fright. 'You can't mean to have me for your dinner! Why, I'm Greedy, your shoemaker friend! I've been watching your pea-patch for you all the morning in your sack!'

Well, you should have seen Big-Eyes stare! His eyes nearly dropped out of his head with surprise when he saw Greedy there instead of Nab. He knew quite well that it was the pixie he had caught – but here was Greedy come out of the sack!

'Of course I won't cook you,' he said at last. 'But I don't understand – I put Nab in the sack for stealing my peas and I meant to punish him by having him for my dinner. How did *you* get there?'

Then Greedy blushed red with shame to think how his stupidity and greed had made him so foolish and put him in such danger. He hardly liked to tell Big-Eyes – but at last he did, and how that giant roared with laughter!

'Ho, ho, ho!' he cried. 'What a joke! So you thought you'd take Nab's job and get the money for yourself – and there wasn't a job and there wasn't any money either! Oh, Greedy, you're like your name, aren't you!'

Greedy stole home ashamed, vowing never to be greedy again. He kept his word – and Nab kept his. So it was a good thing, wasn't it, that Nab was caught that morning, for it certainly changed two people for the better, and gave Big-Eyes the giant something to laugh about for weeks and weeks afterwards!

The Great Big Dog

Willie and Joan were coming home from school one day when they saw, coming round the corner of the lane, a great big dog. It was growling as it came, and the two children looked at it in fright. It was really so very big, and looked more like a wolf than a dog.

'Supposing it's a wolf escaped from somewhere!' said Joan trembling. 'Oh, Willie, have we got time to run away?'

'Let's get into the hedge and perhaps it will pass us by without seeing us,' said Willie. So the two scared children squeezed themselves into the big hedge at the side of the road and crouched there as still as mice.

The big dog came on up the lane. It was limping, the children saw. It held up one of its front paws, and every now and again it licked it as if it was in pain. It didn't seem to see the children, for it came right up to where they were and passed them without a look.

When it had gone a few steps past the big dog

stopped and growled. It lay down in the lane and began to lick its bad foot once more, giving a little whine every now and again as it did so.

'Joan!' whispered Willie. 'It must have hurt its foot.'

'Poor thing!' said Joan. 'Oh, I do hope it goes right on down the lane without seeing us, Willie.'

'But, Joan, do you think we ought to see if we can help it,' whispered Willie. 'We would go up to it if it was a little dog, you know. It's only because it's so big that we don't like it.'

'Oh, no, don't let's go,' said Joan, frightened – but the next minute she changed her mind, for the dog gave another whimper that made the little girl very sorry for it. 'All right – let's go carefully up and speak kindly to it,' she said. 'But please take hold of my hand, Willie.'

Willie took his sister's hand and they came out of the hedge. They walked up to the dog, who looked round at them with a growl.

'Poor fellow, poor fellow!' said Willie. 'Have you hurt yourself? Good dog! Poor old fellow!'

The dog pricked up his ears at the little boy's kind voice and whined. He held up his paw to him. Willie put out his hand but did not touch the dog, for his mother had told him always to let a dog sniff him before he touched it. Then, as soon as he saw the dog wag his tail, he would know the dog was friendly to him, and could touch it.

The big dog sniffed at the small brown hand and then wagged its big brown tail. 'We are friends!' it seemed to say. Willie patted the dog gently and the tail wagged harder. Then Joan patted him, after he had sniffed her hand too, though she was really very much afraid of the big fellow.

'Let me see your poor old paw, then,' said Willie. He took the dog's paw in his hand and held it up. The dog whined again.

Willie turned the paw up to see the underneath of it – and then he saw what the matter was. Run into the pad below the paw were two great thorns, like needles. No wonder the poor creature was in such pain and could not walk on his paw.

'Look, Joan,' said Willie. 'He's got great thorns in his paw. Could you hold the paw while I try to pull them out?'

Joan was sorry to see the dreadful thorns. She held the big paw gently and Willie took hold of one of the thorns. He pulled – and it came out between his finger and thumb. The dog yelped and took away his paw. But Joan took it again and spoke gently to him.

'Don't be afraid, big dog. We're only giving you a little pain to save you from a much bigger one. Keep still while Willie takes out the other thorn.'

The dog cocked his ears, and looked at her with his large brown eyes. He kept his paw still and Willie pulled out the other thorn. There was another yelp, and the dog pulled his paw away. He put it to the ground and found that it no longer hurt him. With a joyful yelp he bounded away down the lane on all four feet, barking as we went.

'Well, he might at least have given us a lick for being kind to him,' said Joan.

'Oh, I expect he wanted to get home,' said Willie. 'I'm glad we were able to do that, Joan. Aren't you?'

But Joan was disappointed in the dog. She thought he ought to have stayed a little with them and showed them he was grateful.

'Oh, don't worry about that, Joan,' said Willie, as they went on their way home. 'He won't forget, you'll see! We can't really expect him to stop and say thank you!'

Now the very next day the two children went into the nearest town to buy a present for their mother's birthday. It was the first time they had gone there alone, and their mother warned

Willie to be careful about crossing the roads, and to look out for motorcars.

'I'll be very careful indeed and look after Joan,' said Willie. So off they went. They bought a fine silver brooch for their mother and then, as they had fifty pence left, they thought they would go to a sweet-shop and buy some chocolate.

'Look! There's a nice sweet-shop over there!' said Joan, and she pointed across the road. 'Let's cross over.'

Willie took her hand and looked up and down the road. 'Wait a moment,' he said, 'there's a motor-car coming.'

'Oh, there's plenty of time to get across!' said Joan impatiently, and she jerked her hand away from Willie's. She ran into the road, and then, oh dear me, she fell over on her nose in the very middle! The car was coming very fast and it could not possibly stop in time. Willie rushed out, but before he could reach Joan, something else had shot past him and had caught hold of the little girl by her frock. It was a great big dog!

He galloped up to Joan, and, without stopping except to grip her dress in his teeth, he shot right across the road in front of the car, carrying Joan with him. The car grazed the dog's tail, but went safely by without touching the frightened little girl. It stopped a little way down the road, and the man at the wheel jumped out. Another man hurried up too – the man who owned the dog.

Joan was frightened but not hurt. She looked at the dog who had saved her, and flung her arms around his neck. 'Oh, you're the same dog we saw yesterday!' she cried. 'We took the thorns out of your foot, and I was cross because you didn't seem grateful. But you didn't forget! And now you've helped *me*!'

The dog's owner was astonished to hear all this, and very proud of his dog. 'He's not much more than a full-grown puppy yet,' he said. 'I'm proud of you, old fellow! You don't forget your friends, I see!'

The dog licked Joan's face and then gambolled over to Willie, who had been very frightened. The little boy went up to Joan and took her hand. 'Come along home,' he said. So Joan went with him, after they had said goodbye to the dog.

'Joan, you mustn't ever do that again,' said Willie, as they went along. 'The dog might not be there another time!'

'I won't do it again,' promised Joan. 'But oh, Willie! Wasn't it a good thing we were kind to the dog yesterday. He saved my life today!'

Get On, Little Donkey!

There was once a small fat donkey who lived in Farmer Brown's field at the bottom of the hill. He had a little shed to live in when it was cold, but he liked being in the field best. Every day Bill, the farmer's boy, used to fetch Neddy the donkey and take him up the hill to work on the farm, for Neddy was strong.

Margery lived on the hillside in a little cottage beside the road up which Neddy and Bill went every day. She liked the donkey and each morning and evening she watched for Neddy and Bill and called to them. Neddy was fond of her for sometimes she held out a carrot to him.

One cold winter's day, when frost was everywhere, and the road up the hillside was coated with ice, Bill went down to fetch Neddy as usual. Twice the boy fell down, for the road was very slippery. Margery watched him from the gate and hoped he wasn't hurt. No – he was not at all hurt, but he was in a very bad temper!

'Bother the ice!' Margery heard him say, angrily. 'It's a perfect nuisance!'

Presently she saw him coming out of the field at the bottom of the hill with Neddy. Neddy needed no guiding, for he knew the way so well. He would always go up the hill by himself, without even a hand on his halter. But this morning he was puzzled and afraid.

His feet seemed slippery. He couldn't walk properly on the road! He didn't know it was because the road was covered with ice. He went slowly up the hill until he was just outside Margery's cottage. Then he stopped, frightened. He felt sure he was going to fall down. He didn't mean to walk another step!

'Get on, little donkey, get on!' shouted Bill. But the donkey wouldn't move an inch.

'Hurry up!' cried Bill. 'We shall be late. What's the matter with you? You know the way!'

The donkey stood perfectly still, his head hanging down, his tail twitching. He couldn't explain to Bill that he was afraid of falling.

Bill became angry. He had no stick with him, for Neddy never needed a stick, but this morning Bill wished he *had* got a stick. He went up to Neddy and slapped him hard on the back.

'Get on, little donkey,' he shouted again. But no – Neddy wouldn't move. He stood as firm as a rock on his four stout little legs.

Bill slapped him again. Then he went to the

donkey's head, took hold of the rope-halter and tugged at it to pull the donkey up the hill. But the donkey was far stronger than he was, and not an inch could the boy move him, one way or another.

Bill was in a fine rage. 'Oh, so you think you'll play a trick on me and make me late for my work, do you!' he cried, angrily. 'Well, we'll see about that! I haven't a stick to beat you with, but perhaps a few stones will make you move!'

Then, to Margery's horror – for the little girl was watching from her gate – Bill went to the side of the road where there were many small stones, and, picking up a big handful, he flung them at the startled donkey. The stones hurt him and he brayed – but he wouldn't move. Bill took up some more stones and threw them with all his might. Neddy brayed again, sadly and angrily. Margery couldn't bear it. It was cruel to throw stones at anything.

'Stop, Bill, stop!' she cried, running out of the gate. 'You're not to hurt him!'

'Well, stones are the only thing to make him go up this hill,' said Bill, sulkily.

'You're right!' said Margery. 'But not used *that* way, Bill.'

'What do you mean?' said Bill. 'How can I use them any other way?'

'I'll soon show you,' said Margery. 'Can't you see the little donkey is afraid to walk on this icy road? I saw *you* fall down on it twice, Bill. This is the way to use the stones, look!'

The little girl ran to the side of the road and picked up two handfuls of the pebbles. She ran to the donkey and spread them under his feet. Then back she went again for more stones, and soon she had made a little pathway of stones for the donkey to walk on. Then she took hold of his halter and spoke kindly to him.

'Get on, little donkey! You're all right now!' The donkey felt the stones under his feet, which no longer slipped on the ice. He took a little step forward. The stones stopped him from slipping. He took another step – and soon he was away from the icy piece, and was walking quickly on the sunny side of the road, where the ice had melted away!

'*That's* the right way to use stones!' said Margery – and Neddy the donkey thought so too!

The Magic Wash-tub

Binny and Tucker were doing their spring cleaning. They had moved all the furniture and scrubbed behind it. They had washed all the chair-covers and banged every book to get the dust out of them. The two pixies had worked very hard indeed, and they were tired.

'Oh dear, we've got to wash all our curtains this afternoon,' groaned Binny, tying her apron strings more tightly round her.

Tucker sighed. He really didn't want to begin washing. If only washing would do itself!

That gave Tucker an idea. 'Binny,' he said, 'do you suppose Dame Sooky would lend us her magic wash-tub for a little while? It would do all our washing for us in about ten minutes!'

'Let's go and ask her!' said Binny. So off the two pixies went. They soon came to Dame Sooky's cottage and rang her bell. Jing-jang, jing-jang!

Nobody came.

'Bother!' said Binny. 'She must be out!'

They went round the back to see if she was in the garden. No, Dame Sooky was not there – but, dear me, something else was! The magic wash-tub was there, on its wooden stand! The magic soap was inside and the scrubbing-brush too.

'Ooh!' said Tucker. 'Look at that! It seems just ready for us to take!'

'Well, let's borrow it, then,' said Binny. 'I'm sure Dame Sooky wouldn't mind! She's a great friend of ours.'

So together they carried the wash-tub home, and stood it in the garden. Then they filled it with hot water and put into it all their dirty curtains.

They stood and watched to see what would happen. In a moment or two the soap jumped up from the bottom of the tub and began to soap the curtains thoroughly. The scrubbing-brush scrubbed the dirt out of them, and then the water soused them up and down just as well as if Binny were doing it herself.

'Isn't it marvellous!' said Binny. 'What a lot of trouble it is saving us! Do you think the curtains are washed enough now, Tucker? Shall we empty out the water and put some fresh in for rinsing?'

'Yes,' said Tucker, and he ran to get the water. Binny emptied out the soapy water, and then Tucker poured in clean water for the tub to rinse the curtains thoroughly.

The tub soused the curtains well. Binny took them out, squeezed them dry and went to hang them up. But just as she had reached the line she heard a cry from Tucker.

'Binny! Look at our mats!'

Binny turned to look – and she saw a strange sight! All her mats and rugs were flapping along in a row to the wash-tub, which was rocking on its stand, and making a most curious noise. The mats flopped in the water and the soap and brush at once began to wash them thoroughly.

Then Binny and Tucker saw something else! They saw all their dresses and suits come marching out of the house in a line, all by themselves! They went to the wash-tub and put themselves in.

'My best dress!' shrieked Binny.

'My best suit!' shouted Tucker, and they ran to the wash-tub to pull out their precious clothes, which were already being well-mixed up with the dirty, dusty rugs and mats!

And then, how they never quite knew, both Binny and Tucker suddenly found themselves pulled into the big wash-tub too! There they were in the hot, soapy water, all mixed up with mats, rugs, suits and dresses!

The soap soaped them well. The scrubbing-brush went up and down poor Binny's arms and nearly scraped the soft skin off them. Tucker was soused under the water and got soap into both his eyes. He opened his mouth to yell and the soapy water ran in.

'Ooh! Ouch!' he spluttered, trying his best to get out of the wash-tub.

Binny's feet were then scrubbed so hard that her shoes came off. She sat down suddenly in the water and the tub nearly went over.

'Oh, oh!' she shrieked. 'Tucker, save me! Oh, I'm drowning! Oh, whatever shall I do?'

The tub soused her up and down well. Then Tucker was soused and rinsed, and he gurgled and gasped, trying to catch hold of the sides of the tub to throw himself out.

Just at that moment an astonished voice cried loudly: 'Binny, Tucker! Whatever are you doing?'

It was old Dame Sooky's voice. She had come in to call on Binny and Tucker on her way home – and she was most amazed to see them jumping up and down in their wash-tub, soaked and soapy. She had no idea at all that it was *her* wash-tub they had borrowed.

'Dame Sooky! D-d-d-dame S-s-s-sooky!' yelled Tucker. 'Help, help!'

Dame Sooky ran across the grass – and at once she saw that it was her wash-tub, and she guessed what had happened.

And then – oh dear – Dame Sooky couldn't help beginning to laugh. She just simply couldn't! It was really too funny to see poor Tucker and Binny being washed and scrubbed in the wash-tub with so many other clothes. She tried her hardest to say the words to stop the tub – but she kept beginning to laugh again.

'Wash-tub, st-st-st –!' she began, and then she laughed again till the tears came into her eyes. 'Wash-tub, st-st-stop your w-w-w-w-washing!' chuckled Dame Sooky – and oh, what a relief, to be sure! It stopped washing poor Binny and Tucker and they were able to climb out of the tub. How queer they looked!

'Oh my, oh my, you'll be the death of me!' laughed Dame Sooky, holding her sides.

'Well, your wash-tub was nearly the death of *us*!' said Tucker, wringing the water out of his coat. 'We'd never have borrowed it if we'd known it would behave like that.'

'You should have waited till I got home, and then I could have told you the words to say to stop it,' said Dame Sooky. 'I never mind lending my wash-tub to my friends, as you know, but not many are so foolish as to take it without knowing the right words to stop it when they want to!'

She took the wash-tub, emptied it, set it on her shoulder and went home with it, laughing so much that a crowd of little elves followed her in astonishment.

As for poor Binny and Tucker they were so tired with their buffeting, soaping and sousing that they took off all their wet things, dried themselves quickly and got straight into bed.

'It would have been easier and quicker to do all the washing ourselves in our own little wash-tub,' said Binny.

'Much easier!' said Tucker. 'We won't be so foolish another time!'

And then, in two twinks, they were fast asleep – and I'm not surprised, are you?

The Lonely Rabbit

Benny was a toy rabbit. He was nearly as large as a real rabbit, and he was dressed in pink striped trousers, a blue spotted coat, a bright orange scarf, and tight blue shoes. So he looked very smart indeed.

But Benny was a lonely rabbit. He belonged to Lucy, and she *would* keep leaving him about everywhere. She left him in the greenhouse one night, all by himself. The next night she left him in the summer-house and spiders walked all over his whiskers and made a web on his pretty blue shoes.

'This is horrid,' said Benny to himself. 'Lucy will keep leaving me alone in these nasty dark places. Why doesn't she remember to take me indoors to the nursery at night, when she goes to bed? She might know that I would like to talk to the other toys. It's a lonely life to be left by myself all day and all night.'

Once or twice Lucy did remember to take Benny indoors and then he was happy. But usually she left him on a garden seat or on the swing, when she went indoors to bed, and then poor Benny was lonely and frightened.

One night Lucy took Benny out into the field just outside her garden. She sat him down beside her and then began to read a book. In a little while some big drops of rain began to fall and Lucy looked up at the sky.

'Goodness!' she said, getting up in a hurry. 'There's a storm coming! Just look at those big black clouds!'

She ran to the garden-gate, opened it and rushed up the garden path. Poor Benny was left sitting in the field!

The rain fell faster and faster. The sky darkened and night came quickly. Benny's coat was soaked through and his pink striped trousers began to run, so that a pink patch showed on the grass around him. His tight blue shoes shrank and burst right off his feet.

'This is dreadful!' said Benny. 'I shall catch a dreadful cold. A-tish-oo! A-tish-oo!'

The rain pelted down and Benny sneezed again. 'A-TISH-OO!'

There was a rabbit-hole just behind Benny. A sandy rabbit suddenly poked the tip of his nose out and said: 'Who's that sneezing? Do come inside out of the rain.'

Benny turned and saw the rabbit. He got to his feet and went to the hole. 'Thank you very much,' he said. 'Do you live here?'

'Of course,' said the rabbit, backing down the hole to make room for Benny. 'This is my home. I say! How wet you are! You *will* catch cold!'

Benny walked down the hole. He was wet and shivering, and he certainly didn't feel very well. The rabbit took him to a cosy room lined with moss and dry leaves.

Another rabbit was there, and she looked at Benny in surprise.

'What are you?' she asked.

'A toy rabbit,' said Benny, and sneezed again. 'A-tish-oo!'

'Goodness, what a cold you've got!' said the second rabbit. 'I think I'd better get Pixie Lightfoot here. She can look after you till your cold is better.'

The first rabbit went to fetch the pixie. She came running in, a merry-eyed creature, with dancing skippitty feet.

'A-tish-oo!' said Benny.

'Goodness, what a dreadful cold!' said Lightfoot. 'Bed's the only place for you. Come with me!'

He followed her down a dark passage and at last came to a cosy room in which were chairs, a table and two small beds.

'Now, undress quickly, and get into bed,' said Lightfoot. 'I'm going to put the kettle on the fire and make you a hot drink.'

Benny took off his dripping pink trousers, his blue coat, and his orange scarf. Then he got into the cosy bed and waited for his hot drink. Oh, it *was* good! It warmed him all over.

'Now lie down and go to sleep,' said Lightfoot. 'Good night!'

'Good – a-tish-oo – night!' said Benny – and in two minutes he was fast asleep.

He was much better in the morning but Lightfoot wouldn't let him get up. No, he must stay in bed until his cold and sore throat were better. She had dried his scarf for him and she tied it round his throat. 'That will keep your throat warm,' she said. 'Now here is some warm milk for you.'

It was lovely to be looked after like that. Benny did enjoy it. It was quite different from being left about by Lucy, who didn't care about him at all. He had plenty of visitors. Both the rabbits came that he had seen the night before, and all their pretty little children. A mole came too and told him a great many stories. Everything was lovely.

Three days later Lightfoot said he could get

up. 'It's a fine sunny day,' she said. 'You can go out of the burrow and sit in the sunshine for half an hour.'

'But suppose Lucy comes to look for me,' said Benny, in alarm. He didn't at all want to go back to her.

'Well, you silly, just pop down the hole again like the other rabbits do,' said Lightfoot. 'You needn't put on your coat and trousers – they have shrunk and are far too small for you – but you must keep on your orange scarf because of your throat.'

So out into the sunshine Benny went, and it was so lovely and warm there that he fell fast asleep. And while he was asleep Lucy came and found him. She lifted him up and looked at him.

'Well!' she said. 'I wonder if this can be Benny. I left him here – but where are his shoes – and his pretty trousers and lovely blue coat? It can't be Benny – but this is his scarf round his neck, that's certain! Except for that he looks very like a real rabbit!'

Just then Benny woke up. He opened his eyes and looked at Lucy. What a shock he got! He struggled and leapt down to the ground. Lucy pounced after him – but he was down the hole in a twinkling, and Lucy couldn't catch him.

'It can't have been Benny!' she thought. 'It

must have been a rabbit that had stolen Benny's scarf – and to think I nearly took him home. Oh, I do wish I could find Benny. I'd never leave him about again if only I could find him.'

But she never did find him – for Lightfoot told Benny he could live with the other rabbits if he liked, and do just as they did. 'It only needs a little magic rubbed into your fur to make you just like them,' she said. 'I'll do it, if you like.'

So she did – and Benny became a real live rabbit like all the rest, as happy as the day was long, with plenty of company and lots to do all the year round.

But Lightfoot made him wear his scarf always, because his soaking had given him a very weak throat, and as soon as he left off his scarf he caught a cold. He always remembers to put it on when he goes out of the burrow, and as it is a very bright orange, it is easy to see.

So if ever you see a rabbit playing on the hill-side, with an orange scarf tied round his throat, you'll know who he is – Benny! But don't tell Lucy, will you?

The Little Bag of Salt

Once upon a time the lion, the tiger, the hyena, the zebra, the ostrich and the snake were all met together. They talked of this and that and then they went to drink at the big water-hole.

Now on the way the lion saw something. It was a small bag and it lay on the ground.

'See!' he said. 'A bag!'

The tiger sniffed at it. 'It smells of salt!' he said.

The hyena tried to untie the string that bound the neck of the bag, but he could not.

'Let the ostrich peck a hole in it,' said the zebra, wisely. So the ostrich pecked a big hole and the salt trickled out. All the animals stood and looked at it.

'I will taste it,' said the snake, and he put out his forked tongue. 'It is salt!' he cried in excitement. 'Salt!'

Then the six animals were most excited for they so seldom tasted salt. It was not to be found anywhere, and was a rare treat. Some man must have dropped this bag of salt and lost it. What a find! Now they would be able to lick salt each day!

'It is mine,' said the lion. 'I saw it first. I shall take it to my cave.'

The tiger growled angrily. 'No,' he said, 'it must be mine. I was the first to sniff it and to tell you all that it was salt!'

'Why should it not be *mine*?' asked the hyena with a sneering laugh. 'Did I not try my best to untie the string?'

'But you failed!' said the quiet zebra. 'It was I who thought of telling the ostrich to peck a hole in the bag. It should be mine!'

'Now come, come!' said the ostrich, stamping her big foot. 'Was it not I who pecked the hole and let out the salt for us all to lick? Surely the bag should belong to *me*!'

'No, no,' said the snake, hissing in rage. 'I tasted it to make sure it was salt. Why, it might have been poison! The salt belongs to *me*! I shall bite anyone who will not let me take it away!'

Then they all began to growl, roar, stamp, hiss and howl, and made such a terrible noise that a little jackal who was running along not far off, stopped in surprise.

'What can be the matter?' he thought. He ran to see, and was most astonished to find the lion,

the tiger, the hyena, the zebra, the ostrich and
the snake all quarrelling noisily round a bag of
salt.

'What are you quarrelling about?' he asked.
The lion told him, and the jackal listened in
silence. Then he scratched his head and
thought.

'I can tell you how to decide who shall have
the bag of salt,' he said, at last. 'Let me hide it
for you, while you all shut your eyes and count
one hundred. Whoever finds it first shall have
it.'

The animals all agreed to do this, for each one
felt certain that he would be clever enough to
find it first. So they all shut their eyes, and
began to count one hundred, as quickly as they
could. They opened their eyes, and began at
once to sniff round eagerly, under the bushes, in
the trees, beneath the rocks.

The lion pawed here and there, the tiger
scraped at the stones. The hyena sniffed, the
zebra snuffed, the ostrich pecked about and the
snake glided under everything. But nobody
could find that bag of salt! It didn't seem to be
anywhere at all!

At last the animals looked at one another,
tired and angry. 'Where's the jackal?' said the
lion. 'We will ask him where he has hidden the

salt, and share it between us! Jackal, come forth! Where is the salt? You shall share it with us.'

But no jackal came forth at all. There was silence everywhere except for the wind that blew. The tiger growled impatiently. 'Jackal jackal, come forth!' he roared.

Still no jackal came – and then the six animals turned and looked at one another. They knew where that bag of salt was now – yes, it was with the cunning jackal, wherever *he* was! But nobody knew his hiding-place!

'Wait till I see that jackal again!' roared the lion – but you may be sure that the jackal kept out of his way for many weeks to come!

Poor Sally Simple!

Once upon a time there lived a dame called Sally Simple. She was very rich indeed, and had fine dresses and wonderful bonnets. She was vain and proud, and always loved to show off her fine clothes and to boast of them.

She lived in Twinkle Village and the folk there disliked her very much.

'If she spent a little of her money on other people, instead of on herself, she would be a nicer person!' they said. But nobody liked to tell Sally Simple this.

Now one day Sally was most excited because she had a new red shawl, new red shoes to match, a wonderful bonnet with red roses on, as light as a feather, and a magnificent sunshade with red roses all round the brim.

'How all the folk in the village will stare when I go out dressed up in my new clothes!' she thought to herself in glee. 'How they will envy me! No one has a sunshade like mine – and no one has such shoes, shawls and bonnets!'

On the next hot, sunny day, Sally Simple dressed herself up in all her new clothes. How grand she looked! Her bonnet was exactly right. Her shoes twinkled in and out as she walked, and very smart they looked. Her shawl was of the finest silk, and as for her sunshade, well it was the prettiest ever seen in Twinkle Village!

All the folk there saw Sally Simple going out in her new finery – and nobody smiled at her, or told her how nice she looked. No – they all turned their heads and looked the other way.

'Look at that mean, vain creature,' said one to another. 'She wouldn't give even a penny yesterday to help poor old Tom Pepper who fell down and broke his leg last week. And now here she is all dressed up in expensive clothes! Well – we just won't look at her or say a single word of praise!'

Sally Simple was annoyed and hurt when no one seemed to see her. She was a foolish woman and didn't know that people thought her mean or vain. So up and down the village she went, holding her head high in its new bonnet, and her new shoes making a clip-clip noise as she walked along.

Now to the village that day came Dame Sly-One, on the look-out for somebody to trick. That was how the rascally old woman got her living. She lived on her wits, and was always picking up money or goods by tricking others not so clever as she was. And as soon as she saw Sally Simple she knew that here was someone she might rob!

'Good morning to you,' she said politely to Sally Simple. 'Could you tell me the way to the tea-shop?'

'Certainly,' said Sally. 'I'm going that way. You can come with me.'

So off they went, the old woman throwing glances of great admiration at Sally's shawl and bonnet.

'I hope you won't mind my mentioning it,' said Dame Sly-One, at last, 'but really, I cannot help remarking what a beautiful bonnet that is you have on – and what a fine shawl!'

Sally Simple was delighted. Here at last was someone who was praising her. She was so pleased that she asked Dame Sly-One to go into the tea-shop and have a cup of coffee with her. So in they went.

They had cups of coffee and buns, and all the time Dame Sly-One was busy praising this and that.

'That bonnet looks rather heavy to me,' she said at last. 'It is very lovely – but surely just a bit heavy to wear, with all those red roses on?'

'Not a bit, not a bit!' said Sally Simple, at once. 'Just try it, Dame. You'll find it is as light as a feather.'

She took off her bonnet and the old dame slipped it on. She looked at herself in the glass and exclaimed in delight. 'Truly beautiful and as you say, as light as a feather! Really marvellous!'

Sally Simple was pleased. 'Doesn't the shawl match the bonnet nicely?' she asked.

'Very well indeed,' said Dame Sly-One, admiringly. 'But it looks to me as if it might be a little too hot.'

'Indeed it isn't!' cried Sally. 'Do you suppose I would choose a hot shawl for this weather! No – it is the coolest shawl I've ever had. Try it and see!'

So Dame Sly-One wrapped the lovely shawl round her shoulders and admired herself in the glass once more.

'It is lovely,' she said, 'and you are again right, my dear Miss Simple. It is not at all hot – in fact, it is a very cool shawl. I might have known that you were clever enough to choose just the right shawl for weather like this!'

'Have you seen the colour of my shoes?' asked Sally, putting out her feet. 'Do you not think they match the shawl beautifully? I had such a task to get them just right.'

'They certainly do match,' said the old dame, 'but it seems to me they look rather uncomfortable to walk in. I don't believe you will be very happy in those, Miss Simple! Pardon my finding fault with such lovely shoes, won't you?'

Sally was not at all pleased. She kicked off her shoes at once. 'Try them on and see for yourself,' she said, quite crossly.

Dame Sly-One put off her own shoes and slipped her feet into the beautiful red pair. 'Do you mind if I just walk up the street a little and try them?' she asked. 'Really, I can hardly believe that such small shoes can be comfortable.'

'Yes, do walk up the street and see,' said Sally eager to make the old dame say she was right. So out of the door went Dame Sly-One, up the street as far as the corner. Then she came back. All the folk of Twinkle Village were most astonished to see her wearing Sally Simple's clothes, and they gaped at her in surprise.

'Once again you are right, dear Miss Simple!' said the old dame, sitting down at the table. 'Really, you have a most beautiful new set of clothes, even to your fine sunshade – though I fear it would not be of much use in the sun! It is very pretty, but would not keep the hot sun off your head very well.'

'You don't know what you are talking about!' said Sally, in quite a temper. 'Why, I chose that sunshade because it is both pretty *and* useful! It keeps the sun's rays from my face in a most excellent way. I beg you to take it and put it up. Go out into the sun and walk a little way. I am sure you will once again come back and tell me I am right!'

Dame Sly-One picked up the sunshade, went to the door and opened it. Then she stepped out into the hot, sunny street, and walked up it, carrying the fine sunshade, and wearing the lovely bonnet, the beautiful shawl and the magnificent shoes. She went right up to the corner, and turned round it.

Sally Simple waited in the tea-shop for the nice old dame to come back. She waited and she waited. When she had waited for ten minutes she became impatient and went in her stockinged feet to the door. She looked out. There was no sign of the old dame at all.

Sally Simple was vexed. She stamped her foot and got red in the face as she always did when she was angry. But still the old dame did not come back.

'Have you seen an old lady anywhere, wearing

my new bonnet, my new shoes, my new shawl, and carrying my new sunshade?' Sally called at last, to some passing shoppers.

'Yes!' they said, grinning. 'We saw her get into her old donkey-cart round the corner there and drive off in a great hurry, looking as grand as a queen! She must have gone off with all your things, Sally Simple!'

Well, of course, that is just what *had* happened. How Sally raged! How she screamed! How she wept! But no one said anything to comfort her at all.

'Sally, you deserve it,' said Mother Trippy. 'Who is going to be sorry that you have lost the fine things that caused you to be so vain, so mean and so proud? Dame Sly-One paid you for them – with flattering words and false praise! You have nothing to grumble at. Go home now, and think about all that has happened and get some good out of it.'

Poor Sally Simple! Home she went in her stockinged feet, with her bare head, no shawl and no sunshade, a sadder and a much wiser woman. And, so people say, she *did* get some good out of Dame Sly-One's trick – for she turned over a new leaf and was much kinder and more generous than she had ever been before. But she is still rather foolish, poor Sally!

Enid Blyton

FIVE O'CLOCK TALES

'Look! Look! There's a bed walking – and there is someone in it!'

A delightful collection of over forty tales. Sneaky the elf steals a growing spell and gets a terrible fright, Snip and Snap the brownies fool the stupid Red Goblin and while Wizard Ten-toes gets out of bed the wrong side, lazy Kate's bed takes her to school!

Enid Blyton

SIX O'CLOCK TALES

'Have you heard me roar?' Snorty asked the elf suddenly, longing to give the cheeky little creature a real fright.

Twinkle the elf isn't afraid of anyone or anything, but when he plays a trick on Snorty the dragon, he gets more than he bargained for! And while Malcolm and Janet go on a thrilling train journey, Tuffy the clown tries to be a hero and Pixie Pinnie paints a cow!

Over twenty-five exciting adventures.

Enid Blyton

EIGHT O'CLOCK TALES

'Who are you? Where do you come from?' the pixie children cried in excitement.

A delightful collection of adventures in which a brave scarecrow foils a plot to kidnap Princess Peronel, two naughty children eat some magic shrinking sweets, and Mollie pays a visit to the old woman who lives in a Shoe, and who makes her doll come to life!

Enid Blyton

NAUGHTY AMELIA JANE!

'Oooh! Look! Your tail has turned into a snake, Teddy!'

Amelia Jane is a very naughty doll. She plays all sorts of nasty tricks on the other toys; she cuts off rabbit's tail, turns poor teddy's plasticine tail into a snake, and pushes the toys out of their snow house. Sometimes they teach her a lesson and she promises to be good, but it doesn't last – Amelia Jane just can't keep out of mischief!

Amelia Jane gets up to more tricks in *Amelia Jane Again!*, *Amelia Jane Gets into Trouble!*, *Amelia Jane is Naughty Again!*

Enid Blyton

AMELIA JANE GETS INTO TROUBLE!

"Oh! Oh! I've knitted myself to the table leg!"

Amelia Jane is a very naughty doll. The other toys hate her tricks. But sometimes they do pay her back for treating them so badly, like the time they tie her to the table-leg with her own knitting and paint her face while she's asleep! If only they could do something about Amelia Jane once and for all . . .

Enid Blyton

THE ENCHANTED WOOD

'Up the Faraway Tree, Joe, Bessie and me!'

Joe, Bessie and Fanny move to the country
and find an Enchanted Wood right on their
doorstep! And in the wood stands the magic
Faraway Tree where the Saucepan Man,
Moon-Face and Silky the elf live. Together
they visit the strange lands which lie at the
top of the tree and have the most exciting
adventures – and narrow escapes!

More magical stories can be found in *The
Magic Faraway Tree* and *The Folk of the
Faraway Tree*.

Enid Blyton

THE MYSTERY OF
THE BURNT COTTAGE

Fatty, Larry, Daisy, Pip, Bets and Buster the dog turn detectives when a mysterious fire destroys a thatched cottage in their village. Calling themselves the 'Five Find-Outers and Dog' they set out to solve the mystery and discover the culprit. The final solution, however, surprises the Five Find-Outers almost as much as Mr Goon the village policeman.

This is the first book in the *Mystery* series.

Enid Blyton

THE MYSTERY OF
THE DISAPPEARING CAT

The Five Find-Outers, Bets, Pip, Daisy, Larry, Fatty and Fatty's dog, Buster, with the help of next door's gardening boy, Luke, try to find out where Lady Candling's prize Siamese cat has gone. It seems that Luke is the chief suspect but the children are sure that he wouldn't have stolen the cat. They have their own suspicions, however – why is Mr Tupping, Lady Candling's gardener, so unfriendly and why won't Mr Goon, the local policeman, listen to them?

The second book in the *Mystery* Series

Enid Blyton

THE SAUCY JANE FAMILY

'Welcome to the Saucy Jane!'

Mike, Belinda and Ann spend their holidays on a beautiful houseboat on the canal – and what an exciting time they have! They learn to swim and have some wonderful holiday treats – like taking a trip on a real canal boat.

Mike, Belinda and Ann have more exciting adventures in *The Seaside Family*.

Enid Blyton

THE TWINS AT ST CLARE'S

Twins Pat and Isabel O'Sullivan are dreading going to St Clare's boarding school for girls. Life is not nearly so easy as at their old school and the 'stuck-up twins' have several unpleasant shocks and arguments before they realise the difficulties are of their own making and settle down and make friends.

Also available in this series:

The O'Sullivan Twins
Summer Term at St Clare's
Second Form at St Clare's
Claudine at St Clare's
Fifth Formers of St Clare's

Enid Blyton

FIRST TERM AT MALORY TOWERS

Darrell Rivers is off to boarding school for the first time. She quickly settles down and makes new friends, including the clever and mischievous Alicia, who delights the form with her practical jokes. But the first term is not all fun and Darrell has some tricky problems to cope with: her dreadful temper, the mystery of Sally Hope's odd behaviour, and the spiteful tricks played on shy Mary-Lou.

Also available in this series

Second Form at Malory Towers
Third Year at Malory Towers
Upper Fourth at Malory Towers
In the Fifth at Malory Towers
Last Term at Malory Towers